"I have asked you to marry me."

He said it with no emotion whatever. "I need an answer."

"I...I..." Laura felt as if she were gasping for air, and the *conde* watched her with a cold intensity. "Why—why me?" she faltered.

"Why not you? I need an heir, and there is no other way to get one. I must marry and have a woman legally in my life," he said brutally. "Marriage is a nuisance, but in your case, it's a nuisance worth facing. I want you very badly."

"I don't understand—"

He walked slowly across to her, standing over her as she sat wide-eyed and trembling. "You understand all too well, señorita. I have desired you from the moment I saw you. Just as you have desired me."

Patricia Wilson used to live in Yorkshire, England, but with her children all grown up, she decided to give up her teaching position there and accompany her husband on an extended trip to Spain. Their travels are providing her with plenty of inspiration for her romance writing.

Books by Patricia Wilson

Bride
of Diaz
Patricia Wilson

Harlequin Books

TORONTO • NEW YORK • LONDON
AMSTERDAM • PARIS • SYDNEY • HAMBURG
STOCKHOLM • ATHENS • TOKYO • MILAN

Original hardcover edition published in 1986
by Mills & Boon Limited

ISBN 0-373-02856-3

Harlequin Romance first edition August 1987

Printed in U.S.A.

CHAPTER ONE

IT was hot, the whole day blazing with that extraordinary light that was characteristic of this part of Spain, a combination of searing heat, clear mountain air and a high, blue, cloudless sky.

Laura stopped her car for a moment to gaze across the clear, shallow river to the mountains beyond. There was more than beauty in their towering height; the high peaks seemed to throw a benediction across the land, a peace that came from their awesome strength, and she breathed a sigh of contentment. She had done the right thing in coming here, she was sure of it. It was a deep feeling of certainty, almost a homecoming.

There was a village some miles away, but she could see it as if it were close at hand. The amazing light seemed to bring everything so close that the white monastery on the distant crags might have been just down the road instead of far away in a village that was probably neither sizeable nor important.

In her drive through Spain she had come to dismiss the impossible and replace it with the thought that it was more than likely. It was a land of magic where the past and present merged, where the dark and the light rode side by side as quiet companions.

A few miles inland from the brash coastal resorts that catered for tourists, the real Spain waited, unchanged in so many ways, shrugging off the mantle of the twentieth century with ease, and she realised as she stared at the distant monastery that she was now very much alone in that older, more romantic Spain.

The thought brought a shiver of excitement and

anticipation, and a glow to her face that would have surprised her former colleagues in England. Sister Laura Marsh, as nervous as any schoolgirl, delighted with the start of an adventure, dreaming dreams of the romantic past. She was almost fiercely glad that she had come, that she had taken a chance and put everything aside to escape from the inevitability of where life was leading.

She started the engine and her brilliantly blue eyes turned to the sparkling river that gushed over the stones of the shallow ford. Once across, she would be approaching the mountains, travelling on a road that led through huge forests of pine and Spanish oak, the beginning of the vast Montanas estate where she would be working for the foreseable future. It would be very different from her work in the busy hospital in London, and she was not without some inner fears as she turned the car on to the narrow road that ran like a white ribbon up into the foothills before disappearing into the trees.

From here, the forest seemed dark, forbidding, alarming, but the sunshine was hot on her arms, it caught the astonishing fairness of her hair, turning it almost to silver. She drove slowly across the ford, her delicate and beautiful face set in the lines of determination that her friends knew so well. She would face whatever lay ahead of her. She had come here with her eyes wide open and nothing could be so frightening as the prospect of a marriage that was slowly and inevitably being forced on her by well-meaning friends and by David.

She needed time to think, to look at things from another angle, and here was certainly a place which would shake her out of any lethargy that had been slowly strangling her. She would know soon enough if her affection for David was merely the warm feeling that a long friendship brought, or if it was love. Perhaps she was wrong to expect more from love than a quiet feeling of companionship, but she was not prepared to marry and then discover that she had made a mistake.

She was not even sure how it had come about that the whole hospital spoke of herself and David in one breath. Doctor Elliott and Sister Marsh. It was the urging of David towards marriage and the almost determined acceptance of the reality of it by friends and colleagues that had finally decided her course of action.

When the advertisement in *The Times* had caught her eye, she had applied with little hesitation. Nurse and companion to a Spanish Condesa; a little out of Laura's line, but she was accustomed to dealing with patients who had heart problems and it would give her time to think. Spain was far away from Central London.

Almost too far away, she had thought more than once on the long drive through France. The firm of solicitors who had interviewed her in London had assumed that she would wish to avail herself of the first-class ticket offered and would fly out to Spain. They had been somewhat astounded when she had informed them that she intended to take her own car and drive out to southern Spain. But she had holiday due to her and she wanted as many things of her own with her as possible. Inner caution advised her to have her own means of transport and, looking now at the forbidding darkness of the trees, she wondered if her instincts had been to keep to herself the means of a possible speedy retreat.

But the forest when she entered it was not the menacing spectacle that it had appeared to be when she had observed it from below. The trees were widely spaced and there was plenty of hot Spanish sunshine to fill the little clearings. She relaxed and the drive became once again a pleasure, part of her holiday, soon to end as she started her new duties.

Something caught her eye halfway down the wooded hillside. A castle. Its position and beauty were breathtaking, and she braked the car as a gasp of pleasure left her lips.

High walls and turrets stood pale gold in the sunlight. Great arched windows and stone balconies studded its face and, though it seemed far away, its beauty held her spellbound for minutes, as though it was an enchanted place.

Its lower walls hidden in the greenery of the nearer forest, the castle seemed to rise from the trees like a mirage, almost hovering and faintly luminous in the very special light of the mountains.

A strange feeling came over Laura as she sat entranced. Somehow she recognised that the sight of it was an event in her life, like a beacon of light. Wherever she had been going, she would not have been able to ignore its call, but she realised with a growing feeling of excitement that this must be the Castle of Fire, Castillo del Fuego, her destination and the home of the aristocratic Montanas family for generations. Mr Bloom, of Messrs Bloom, Bloom and Rudley, had been almost awestricken in his tones when he had spoken of them; his office had taken on the barbaric splendour of Spain's turbulent past as he recounted their history in hushed tones.

Laura had been left in no doubt that to work for them was a great honour, that her performance would reflect on the old firm of solicitors who represented the count in England—who had 'the honour' to represent the count.

Her amusement at the time was now not so uppermost in her mind. She could understand just what he had been feeling and she wondered vaguely if he had ever been here, if he had had 'the honour' to be invited to the *castillo*.

The desire to sit there all day and gaze at it was very strong, but duty was stronger. Tomorrow she would be expected to start and she had no doubt that she would be expected to start well. She bit her lip when David's final angry words came into her mind.

'You realise what you're doing, I suppose, Laura? You've given up a great deal of authority by resigning from the hospital. There'll be no authority for you there, my girl. You've signed yourself on as nothing more than a servant in this posh Spanish household. A paid companion and nurse to hold the hand of some complaining and doddering countess. It isn't going to last long when you realise what you've given up. There'll be no "Yes, Sister. Right away, Sister Marsh". When you get there you'll be in a totally subservient position, probably with a room in one of the turrets.'

Well, there were plenty of turrets; she would have to see. Laura started the car and moved off, her mind swimming with impressions and memories, caught between the real world she had left and the glimpse of magic that the castle and the very land itself had afforded. She hardly knew now whether she had done the right thing in coming here. She could as easily have left the hospital and gone to another one, to a place where she would not have David pushed at her from morning until night until she hardly knew her own mind any more.

Certainly the grandeur of the castle had unnerved her a little, even though the sight of it had given her a strange uplift of spirit. She turned her head for one last look, and it was a mistake. The front wheel of the car hit a rock that she had not seen and alarm filled her mind as momentarily the steering wheel was jerked from her hands to spin uselessly to the left.

She had regained control in a second, but not soon enough, because the car was heading rapidly for a huge ditch beside the narrow road and there was nothing that she could do to prevent it. It plunged in nose first and Laura's head rocked sickeningly with the impact before the car came to rest in a stranded and ungainly position, its radiator against the trunk of one of the giants of the forest, its back wheels spinning wildly.

She turned off the engine and sat for a second feeling shocked and lightheaded. As an accident, it was only a minor happening, but she was well aware that a very large shock could come from a very small accident. Even seated, her legs felt woolly and from the pain in her head she knew that she would be starting her duties tomorrow with a large bruise on her forehead that no white starched cap would hide.

There was a thunder of sound and she turned her head, struggling to move and at the same time almost tearfully frustrated when she discovered that the door was well and truly jammed.

'*Estate quieto!*'

The voice cracked like a whip across the sunlit clearing and Laura turned dazed eyes towards the sound, gulping down the scream that rose in her throat.

There was a man coming towards her fast. The thundering had been the sound of his horse, a huge black beast that was being urged through the trees with no regard for the thick overhanging branches, the rider bending almost casually in the saddle to avoid them.

Laura's eyes widened with growing fear as the horse plunged closer, but it was not the colour or the size of the animal that alarmed her, it was the man himself.

His clothes were black, his shirt fitting sleekly across his chest, the full sleeves tight at the wrists. A flat-brimmed black sombrero shaded the dark face from her eyes, and she felt a burst of fear that was both instinctive and superstitious.

It showed clearly on her face, and his lips tightened with annoyance as he leapt from the horse to stride over to her.

'The—the door's jammed. I—I'm stuck!'

She struggled to regain her composure, but she had

never felt quite like this before in her life and he could see clearly the effect that his presence was having on her.

'I can well imagine that it would be,' he said shortly. 'I will get you out. There is a very strong smell of petrol and the sun is hot. I would not wish to see you trapped like a pigeon in an oven, *señorita*.' His voice crackled with savagery and his dark presence seemed to fill the clearing as if he had materialised on a clap of thunder and should vanish in the light of the sun. Laura gasped at the callous words, said so easily, and a feeling of outrage took the place of her growing fear of him.

'I really think . . .'

'Be quiet! I must get you out.' His harsh voice silenced her into instant obedience. The fact that he spoke English with only the faintest trace of accent was no comfort. She found her mind tossing wildly between fantasy and reality. He seemed, like the castle, to have come from some past time, a time when the knights were as terrifying as the infidels they fought. The intensity and the coldness of the days of El Cid was in his gaze and she half expected to see him joined by horsemen of another age.

He stepped sideways and a powerful black-booted foot lifted and slammed into the door handle, which gave immediately—and who wouldn't? she thought on a rising wave of hysteria, still sitting there, staring into his face with alarm racing through her.

'You are free, *señorita*.' For seconds the glittering black eyes looked down into hers and she was hypnotised by a haunting fear at the stillness of him. The cold aristocratic face had not softened and had shown no sign of any emotion even though he had apparently been convinced that the car might at any time explode into flame. It was a handsome face, harsh and forbidding, with high cheekbones, straight nose and straight black brows.

The smell of petrol was now strong and the thought of a possible explosion had Laura struggling to get out. The car was at a very odd angle and getting out proved to be rather difficult, but he simply stood back and watched her, making no attempt to help, even though he could see that she was shocked and dazed.

Annoyance brought a flush to her cheeks, a flush that deepened as her efforts had her skirt rising well above her knees and his night-black eyes flickered down the slender length of her legs and then upwards to the feminine curves of her body, ill-concealed by the thin summer dress of blue voile.

She managed to struggle upright in spite of his disturbing proximity and the unnatural angle of the car, but no sooner did her feet touch the ground than her legs folded under her in an alarming feeling of helplessness and she would have fallen but for the strong arms that scooped her up.

'Ah! I expected that you would have difficulty in remaining upright, *señorita*. I would have lifted you out, but your expression led me to believe that your screams would have been heard at the *castillo* had I so much as laid a finger on you.'

He held her against his chest, a chest as iron-strong as his arms, and for a second looked down into her eyes.

'You are incredibly fair,' he murmured almost to himself. Her pale hair spilled over his black sleeve and he looked at it with astonishment. 'Your hair is like spun silver in the sunlight. You have eyes like sapphires,' he added, his dark eyes searching the beauty of her face. 'Light and dark, you and I. *Sol y sombra*.'

He stopped speaking abruptly, a frown creasing his forehead as if he had angered himself by his momentary lapse into poetic speculation.

'Come, we are still too close to the car, although I now very much doubt if there is danger. However, we must get you to the hospital; it is not too far. You have taken a hefty bump on your head, I think, and you are rather shocked.'

Laura felt that any shock was due almost in its entirety to the dark disturbing presence of her rescuer and his indifference to her predicament. She was astounded that he was sufficiently interested in her well-being as to suggest that she see a doctor.

'I'm perfectly all right now, *señor*. You may put me down,' she said as firmly as her trembling lips would allow.

'I think not,' he returned flatly, and strode off with a finality that left her gasping.

'Wait!' Laura struggled, uselessly as it turned out, but at least he stopped. 'I can walk; there's no need whatever to carry me. And what about my luggage?' she added breathlessly when he showed not the slightest intention of releasing her.

He seemed completely unmoved and looked down into her face with a derisive smile.

'It is my intention to carry you only as far as Diablo, *señorita*. And there is no need to look at me with eyes like saucers; I refer to the horse, not, as you seem to imagine, to my master.'

'Can't—can't we get my car started?' Laura stammered, unnerved again by his astute assessment of her opinion of him.

'It is in a ditch, *señorita*. I am strong, but I have never been required to take the place of a breakdown truck. It is not my intention to start now!'

'But the horse! Couldn't we fasten a rope ...' Her voice faltered at the look of angry disapproval that was aimed at her like a black arrow.

'Diablo is a thoroughbred Arab stallion, a miracle of fine bone and muscle with the speed and beauty of the eagle and the fire of the desert sun in his nostrils. He is not a dray horse! I would not risk either his superb body nor his uncertain temper by requiring that he should dislodge your car from the hapless position that it now occupies!'

He strode forward again, and Laura felt duly chastised.

'At least could I get my handbag? My luggage is locked in the boot. I expect it will be all right.'

'It will, *señorita*. You are on the Montanas estate. All and sundry do not wander here and anyone who does is not likely to be carrying duplicate keys.'

'You were wandering here, *señor*,' Laura shot at him quickly, and earned herself a slanting glance of dark-eyed reproof.

'Luckily for you, *señorita*. As it happens, I have every right to wander here. In fact, wandering here is part of my duties.'

'You—you work at the castle?' She wondered what job could be found to occupy someone so haughty and arrogant as this dark stranger with a skin burnished by the sun and hair like a blackbird's wing.

'I do, and for the moment I will not ask your reasons for wandering on to Montanas land. Let us simply get you to the hospital where one of the *médicos* can take a look at you.'

'I don't need a doctor, *señor*. I'm not injured and I know perfectly well how I feel. I'm a nurse.'

'A nurse!' For the first time she felt that her words had his full attention. 'What is your name?' He rapped out the question like one accustomed to giving orders, and Laura felt a stab of misgiving as he suddenly set her on her feet and glowered down at her.

'Laura Marsh. I doubt if that means anything to you, *señor*.'

'But it does, *señorita*. You are the nurse who is to be companion to the Condesa, *es verdad?* Sister Marsh, I believe?' He eyed her with dark disapproval. 'Someone older and—more substantial was expected. You are too slender to be capable of the work required and you are far too young. It would appear that qualifications are easily obtained in England if one so young and fragile can indeed be a nursing Sister!'

His insolence took her breath away, but only momentarily.

'I'm twenty-four, *señor*, and size is not synonymous with efficiency! I've been thoroughly investigated by the Conde's lawyers in England and I can't see that any of this concerns you. To satisfy you, however, I would let you read my qualifications but I do not normally need to keep them pinned to my person!' Her tone said clearly that she doubted his ability to read in any case, and his face darkened even more.

'You have the tongue of an angry gypsy girl, Sister Marsh! You become more unsuitable with every passing moment.'

'How do you know about me?' Laura demanded sharply. 'My business is with the Conde and the Condesa. I sincerely hope I will not have to prove my nursing abilities to every worker on the estate!'

'Your arrival is awaited with, shall we say, baited breath, Sister Marsh,' he explained, his tightened lips relaxing into a sardonic smile. 'The whole of the Castillo trembles in anticipation. I believe that they have been polishing the brasses and setting their beds at right angles to the walls. It has, I believe, been explained to them that you will not be carrying out a daily check on all the bedrooms and that you will not necessarily pace the corridors at night carrying a lamp, but still they tremble. Here in the mountains we are a simple people, *señorita*. A nursing Sister from England is looked upon with a certain amount of awe. What they will make of your slender beauty and silver hair I cannot think. Certainly they will find it hard to take you seriously. I very much doubt whether you will last long in the post, even if you are permitted to begin.'

His tone and the amused curl of his lips infuriated Laura no less than the slightly breathless feeling that being in his arms had brought.

'I'm a nurse, not a field-marshal, *señor*!' she snapped. 'And whether I'm unsuitable or not is absolutely nothing to do with you! I would be grateful if you would allow me to get my bag so that we can continue to the castle.'

'*Momento*,' he said softly, and then she was swinging through the air to be placed lightly but firmly on the great black horse.

Diablo liked it no more than she did, and Laura had a glimpse of rolling eyes and a definitely wicked expression as he turned his head. It removed her other anxiety, that her skirt was once again well above her knees.

'*Tranquilo, tranquilo.*' The man spoke softly, his hand on the gleaming neck, and there was instant stillness from the animal. 'I will get your bag.' He was back in seconds to hand it to her before swinging effortlessly into the saddle behind her. 'I had better hold you, I think. I hope you will not take this as a further sign of my insolence, *señorita*?' There was a soft anger in his voice, but she didn't care. The sooner she was away from this irritating man and into the castle the better. She was, in fact, too annoyed to have more than a slight feeling of unease at the isolation of her position in the forest and the utter stillness that surrounded them when their voices were silent.

'I'm perfectly all right!' There was a decided feeling that she had to get her words out fast before he took some further drastic action, and she couldn't help but compare his arrogant manner with the kindliness of David. If David had been rescuing someone he would have behaved very differently. This autocratic Spaniard clearly thought that she needed medical attention, and yet the thought had not prevented him from stopping to hurl insults at her and interfere in her affairs. She could have been dying of internal injuries for all he knew while he was angrily discussing things that were none of his business.

'I was not thinking of you, *señorita*, so much as Diablo. You remain here safely only because it was I who placed you on his back. He is unaccustomed to carrying anyone other than myself and is as yet undecided as to how he should react to this strange turn of events.'

Laura could see what he meant. The horse was as taut as a bowstring, his ears laid flat to his head, so when a strong arm encircled her waist, drawing her back against the hard chest and thighs of her rescuer, she kept silent. Naturally he had been thinking about the horse and not her, she thought angrily. He probably got on better with the great brute than with human beings; no wonder that he had no way of knowing how to behave! It was probably his job to run the forest and he probably never came out of it. It was a miracle that he even remembered how to talk at all; how he came to be able to speak such good English was another thing. The thought puzzled her and gave her some inner misgivings. Clearly he was educated. An educated savage! An impossible man.

She could not, however, prevent a slight shiver of excitement and fear at the power of the superb male body and the strong arm that held her in safety, and her cheeks flushed when he again said softly, '*Tranquilo*.' She didn't know whether he was addressing her or the horse, but the low dark chuckle that followed the words left her with the strong impression that the advice to calm down was not addressed to Diablo. He may have been only a worker on the estate, but he was too much of a man to be ignored totally and she hoped she would not be obliged to see him again. He had reduced her to angry trembling when she

knew perfectly well that her affairs did not in any way
concern him.

The castle was closer than Laura had imagined, and soon
her misgivings eased as she saw that they were indeed
travelling in the right direction. The smooth rhythm of
the horse, the strangely comforting power of the body
behind her and utter safety of the arm that held her close
almost lulled her to sleep after the shock of her accident
and her rage with the Spaniard, and she found herself
relaxing against him as they rode through clearings
dappled with sunlight. It was almost with a shock of
regret that she sat upright as they began to plunge
downwards through soft grass and undergrowth to the
level of the castle itself.

'You are safe.' The deep, quiet voice seemed to fit so
well into the peace and grandeur of the scenery that
Laura forgot for a moment to be irritated. 'Diablo is sure-
footed. We are not about to be unseated. You may relax
again.'

Hardly the words to allow her to continue in
tranquillity. He had noticed that she had leaned against
him and she was glad that her clouds of hair hid her swift
rise of colour. One moment's peace and he was away
again, irritating, insolent, arrogant!. She held herself
uncomfortably upright for the rest of the ride, ignoring
the certain feeling that he was laughing at her, no doubt
adding her femininity to the mounting list of her failings.

If she had sought the spectacular, their entrance into the
courtyard of the Castle of Fire would have been all that
she could have hoped for. The sound of the horse, his
hooves ringing on the stones as they rode under an arch
that seemed to date from the days of the *conquistadores*,
was a signal of their arrival as loud and clear as a bell and
it brought forth two servants instantly.

'My car, *muy rápido*!' The man snapped out the words as he swung smoothly from the horse, lifting Laura to the ground and turning the animal over to one of the men. 'Give me your keys, *señorita*,' he added quietly. 'When we come back from the hospital your luggage will be here and I will arrange to have your car removed and repaired.'

She wanted to tell him to go away and try to mind his own business, but everyone else was obeying him and he was at that moment not a man to argue with. She handed him her keys with a speed that astonished her and in turn they were handed to one of the men as a rapid conversation ended with the man saying,

'*Sí*, Señor Conde.'

Laura just stared at him and never moved even when his car was brought up with the speed he had ordered and he stood with the passenger door open, looking at her with raised eyebrows and quizzical expression.

'You—you are the Conde?' It was hard not to be open mouthed.

'*Sí, señorita*,' he said smoothly, his eyes cold and hard. 'Rodrigo Estéban Diaz, Conde de las Montanas, at your service and waiting to take you to the hospital.'

He motioned to the car, but Laura stood her ground.

'It was quite despicable of you not to tell me who you were, Señor Conde!' she accused angrily. 'You allowed me to assume that you were interfering in things that did not concern you. It was hardly the action of a gentleman.'

'Possibly not,' he said with smooth disdain, his eyes cold, 'but it enabled me to discover so much more than I would have found out in a quiet little chat that is so beloved of the English. You revealed several things that are not at all to my liking, but we will discuss them later. The hospital is, I think, the first item that should be dealt with.'

He motioned to the car again, but Laura simply stood

still and stared at him with dislike.

'There's no necessity for this, Señor Conde. I'm perfectly capable of judging the state of my health. I've come here to do a job, and I would now be obliged if you would take me to see your wife.'

'That would be difficult, *señorita*,' he said softly, leaning against the car as if he had all the time in the world and had every intention of being obeyed. 'I am not married. The Condesa is my mother and she will be your patient if you remain, but I am not about to present you to her at this moment. You have a bruise on your forehead, your dress is less than bandbox-fresh and you have an unlikely flush on your pale cheeks. You have clearly been in an accident and perhaps the Condesa will have the same thoughts that have been in my mind since I discovered your identity. How can you be expected to care for someone whose health is uncertain when you cannot even look after yourself? It does not lead one to great confidence regarding your capabilities, apart from your other failings.'

'You are insulting, Señor Conde!' Laura wished her legs would stop shaking; she would walk inside and defy him. She would introduce herself to the Condesa!

'Merely speculating, Sister Marsh. Shall we go?' He held the car door wide open and she had no alternative but to obey, a fact that gave him no apparent satisfaction. He was accustomed to being obeyed and his every movement said it clearly as he rounded the bonnet of the car with the easy strides of a jungle cat and slid into the driving seat.

'You will find this ride not so unnerving perhaps as the ride on Diablo. Let us hope that you do not continue to be so agitated,' he observed cynically, making her seeth with rage. Agitated now! Her faults were endless!

'I'm grateful that you rescued me, Señor Conde,' Laura

said sharply, mutiny on her face, ' but I don't recall being agitated.'

'As I have already intimated, you are far too young for the post,' he said with infuriating calm. 'Normally, your agitation would have merely brought out my protective instincts, but this, Sister Marsh, is no normal situation; you are proposing to care for my mother, the Condesa. If you have any hospital discipline at all, it certainly deserted you on the ride through the forest. I had expected an efficient nursing Sister, accustomed to taking responsibility and making decisions.' He shot her a look of cool disdain. 'You are merely a woman; barely that, a girl almost.'

'I have the qualifications, efficiency and hospital discipline of any sister twice my age, Señor Conde. However, if you require a nurse for your mother of more ample proportions, I will try to improve my appetite!' She managed to convey that it would be difficult to have any appetite at all, living in the *castillo* with him, and he took the point quickly, his dark face darkening even further. 'And I am well aware that I am a woman, thank you; in fact, I am engaged to be married!'

She threw the remark at him with what she hoped was the force of an Olympic javelin thrower, and it had the desired effect. His hand stilled as it reached out to the ignition and he looked across at her swiftly.

'Engaged to be married? You wear no ring, *señorita*. I had imagined that it was the unfailing custom in your country that every girl required diamonds, that some even became engaged merely for the ring when the man himself had little appeal for them.'

'We—we're not officially engaged yet. We have an— understanding.' Laura wished he would look away. His eyes seemed to be pinning her to the pale leather seat of the long cream-coloured Mercedes and she had the uncomfortable feeling that he was prying into her mind.

'An understanding—I see. He must be very understanding! Who is this paragon of virtue who allows you to desert him and try your hand at a new and unsuitable venture before taking you under his wing to tame you?' He was looking at her as if she was a very wayward child and her annoyance grew at the same time as her embarrassment.

'In England women do not marry in order to be tamed, Señor Conde,' she pointed out tartly.

'A fact which may account for your climbing divorce rate. If you deserted me I would bring you back most speedily and spank you soundly,' he added with a smugness that infuriated Laura.

'When I leave the Castle of Fire, Señor Conde, it will not be desertion, it will be as the result of my resignation!'

She glared at him and he raised dark mocking eyebrows.

'Perhaps it would be less complicated for all of us if you were to resign now, Sister Marsh,' he suggested nastily, 'although I suppose it would be best if you were to see the Condesa first. She may even like you,' he added, conveying that this would be most unlikely. 'She is totally unlike me. She is English.'

'English?' Laura could hardly believe her ears. There could surely be no English blood in the veins of this proud dark-skinned man who now drove with skill and speed along the main highway.

'Sí, English. You have my assurance and, in any case, you will see for yourself very soon. She does not have your dazzling fairness, but she was, and still is, very beautiful.' He shrugged elegantly. 'I suppose that you could say that I am half English, although I do not feel it. A strange likeness runs in my family that has been recognisable for generations and, as you will see when you look at the portraits in the castle, it continues even in me. The

Montanas genes are too powerful to be subdued. I look as my father looked and his father before him. Centuries of similarity. You find that boring, Sister Marsh? You are searching for something different, while the Montanas are anxious to remain always the same.'

'No, I find it fascinating.' For a moment Laura forgot to be angry, gazing with wide-eyed interest at the dark, handsome face, the heavy black hair, the thick, curling black lashes that brushed his cheeks as he looked down. He was, she supposed, the most handsome man she was ever likely to meet; the most ruthless, too, probably; decidedly the nastiest!

He tipped his black sombrero forward on his face and leaned back comfortably in the leather seat. His hands were strong and skilled, quite beautiful, his eyes narrowed against the glare of the sun, and she was so enthralled that she actually jumped when he looked across at her suddenly with dark intent eyes.

'And what conclusions have you drawn from your inspection of me, *señorita*?'

'I was thinking you would make a very irritating patient, Señor Conde,' she lied charmingly, her face dimpling into a smile, the first time he had seen her in anything but an angry or frightened moment.

'You believe so?' His eyes moved quickly over her face before returning to the road and he smiled too, showing strong, even, white teeth. 'I will try never to be ill if after all you are to remain here. I would not like you to vent your annoyance on me from the other end of a hypodermic needle.'

'I would never hurt you, Señor Conde,' she assured him sweetly, relishing the thought of having him at her mercy, and his eyes narrowed even further as he stared at the long road ahead.

'I doubt if anyone could, *señorita*,' he asserted coldly,

ending the conversation, his aristocratic face perfectly
still and expressionless.

CHAPTER TWO

AFTER the towering splendour of the ancient castle, the hospital was a shock and a revelation to Laura. It stood beside the main road a few miles from the *castillo* and it was not, as she had imagined it would be, some old building hastily renovated; every stone was spanking new and painted brilliantly white. The fresh green of newly planted lawns surrounded it and it was clear that money and care had been poured into it.

Without having even stepped through the doors, Laura was impressed and, once she was through the heavy swing doors, her approval grew in leaps and bounds. It was a small but modern hospital, everything bought within the last few years; equipment here that they had been striving to get at St Mark's for months and months.

'It meets with your professional approval?'

The Conde looked down at her with a superior smile, but she could hardly disagree. There was a calm efficiency about the place that certainly met with her approval, and she marvelled that such a place existed so far into the mountains.

'Ah, Doctor Hernandes.' The Conde's face lost none of its coldness as he greeted the man who came forward from one of the side wards. Perhaps it was because he was so very different from the Conde, Laura thought nervously. Whatever the reason, there was an added chill in the air as introductions took place with the usual Spanish courtesy.

'This is Señorita Marsh, Dr Hernandes,' the Conde said stiffly. 'Actually, she is Sister Marsh, and no doubt

25

you will find that you have a lot in common. However, the merits of various hospitals can be discussed later, if she stays. For now, she has had an accident on the way to the *castillo*, and I would be obliged if you would examine her and see whether or not she has suffered any real damage.'

For a second, Laura's blue eyes met the smiling kindness of Doctor Hernandes. His deep brown eyes were warm and intelligent and a look of understanding flared between them that made her want to almost weep with relief. All Spaniards were not like the Conde; she had met a friend and helper who understood her predicament without any words having been spoken. He was an oasis of calm.

She went willingly when he motioned her to the same side ward that he had just left, gleefully pleased that the Conde made no move to follow and that the doctor shut the door with a firm hand.

'Sit down, Sister Marsh, and tell me about your injuries.' He was laughing quietly, and she sank with relief into the nearest chair.

'I have no injuries, Dr Hernandes, except perhaps to my pride.'

'I know the feeling,' he grinned. 'When one battles with the Conde one is in a no-win situation every time. What happened?' She told him, quickly and easily. It was so nice to talk to someone near normal after a time in the Conde's company.

'*Bueno!*' He straddled a chair that he had pulled up close. 'We will just check, in case. And then we will pass the time talking shop. I am not sure whether the Conde will be fooled, but at least a sufficient time will have passed to ease his suspicions. However, you are probably all right.'

He produced a small torch, and, as he tested her

reflexes, examined her pupils and grunted with satisfaction, they talked.

'You were startled, no doubt, to see this hospital so far into the mountains?'

'I was. It looks as if money is no object. I wish we had some of the equipment in St Mark's that you have here.'

'Yes, we are lucky and, as you say, money is no object. The Conde set this hospital up a few years ago and we are improving it all the time.'

'The Conde!' Laura was utterly surprised. 'So that there will be a hospital close by for his mother?'

'Oh no, Sister Marsh. I honestly do not think that the thought entered his head for one moment. In spite of his rather dramatic appearance and his desire to have his own way in every way, he really cares for the people. He has worried for some time about the distance of some of the villages to good medical facilities and when, several years ago, a child in San Fredo almost died in an accident, he determined that we would have a hospital here. When the Conde determines something, it always happens,' he added with a smile. 'He lured me from Madrid with a salary that I could hardly believe, and together we planned this hospital. It was an exciting venture; it still is and, oddly enough, he never interferes, simply pours money into it when it is needed. The people of the mountains and the nearby valleys would be in considerable distress were it not for the Conde's generosity.'

'How did you know him?' Laura couldn't imagine how Doctor Hernandes could have become known to the Conde, but the explanation was obvious really.

'The Condesa' he said quietly. 'She has been in hospital in Madrid several times and I was treating her at one time. He remembered me, that is all.' He laughed drily at her expression. 'You are thinking that he doesn't even like me? You are wrong, Sister Marsh. We have an ongoing battle, the Conde and I. His mother is gravely ill, and I hope you realise the extent of the responsibility that you have taken upon your slim shoulders. She could die at any time,' he sighed, 'and yet there is no need for it. A bypass operation could restore her to almost normal health. There is, in her case, a fifty-fifty chance, but the Conde will not hear of it, and I cannot let the matter drop. Therefore, from time to time, we clash. I need not tell you, I think, that the Conde always wins.'

'What does the Condesa think?' Laura asked anxiously.

'She knows the risk, but she would take the chance in order to live a more normal life. However, she will not upset her son, and he is of the opinion that if she has the best of care, she will live a normal life span. He is wrong. Your appointment here is, shall we say, a compromise.'

'A compromise?'

'Yes. The Condesa feels that your presence will, how shall I say, restrict her activities? She does many things that she should not, gardening for example; the gardens at the *castillo* are the joy of her life. The Conde cannot watch her all the time and she feels, I know, that part of your duties will be to report to her son when she has been—er—disobedient?'

'Oh!' Laura felt outraged. If the Conde was expecting her to act as a spy he had another think coming! She looked up to find the doctor regarding her with amusement.

'Ah! Perhaps this time Rodrigo Estéban Diaz, Conde de las Montanas, has bitten off more than he can chew. I see the light of battle in your eyes, Sister Marsh.'

He swung effortlessly to his feet, a man slightly younger than the Conde, she thought, and handsome too, though not perhaps with the same compelling looks as the Conde.

'I appear to be already battling with the Conde,' Laura

said ruefully. 'Apparently I'm too young and too slim. I shudder to think what he expected or what type of nurse would meet with his approval.'

The doctor grinned down at her and seemed not one bit surprised.

'Keep battling, Sister Marsh,' he advised. 'But let us join him now before he bursts in and finds that we are simply chatting.'

'Surely he wouldn't dare?'

'He would dare anything, Sister Marsh,' the doctor assured her. 'He is the Conde de las Montanas and the wild and often violent blood of his ancestors runs in his veins. I would not like to bank on anything to such an extent that I would be prepared to say that he would not do it. He is fearless in all things and arrogant in most. If he wishes to do something, you may be assured, he will!'

The Conde appeared to be quietly fuming when they joined him, and Laura was glad that they had not chatted longer. The man was putting all her nerves on edge in a way that no one had every been able to do before.

'Well?' The snapped out question did not appear to ruffle the doctor in any way, and he informed the Conde that, apart from a bruised forehead that would mend rapidly, Sister Marsh was in excellent health.

'Excellent? She is pale as a moonbeam!' The Conde looked at both of them as if there was a conspiracy to keep her terminal ill health from him. 'She looks barely capable of standing upright!'

'It is her nature, Señor Conde, her genes. She looks pale and delicate. You are dark and strong. We are all at the mercy of our genes and her delicate appearance is nothing. She is in good health and no doubt strong, otherwise she would not have survived as a nurse long enough to reach the position of Sister.'

The Conde looked doubtful and not pleased either that she was stronger than she looked, but he glowered and

ushered her out, clearly displeased to have his opinion of
her challenged by the doctor.

There was an oppressive silence in the car on the way
back to the castle, and Laura found herself growing more
uneasy by the minute. She had met many consultants of
uneven temper during her career, but their stay on the
wards had been brief. This man was going to be part of
her life for some considerable time and she was rapidly
finding herself at a loss as to how to deal with him.

'I think I need to talk to you about my duties, *señor*,'
she said into the deep silence, her remarks more to break
the uncomfortable gloom that seemed to have descended
than to elicit any immediate information.

'You are to be *compañera* to my mother, your nursing
skills to be used when required.' His answer was brief,
almost surly, and he seemed to think that no other words
were necessary.

'I realise that, *señor*. I'm at a loss, though, as to why you
required a Sister. Surely any registered and experienced
nurse would have been suitable?'

'You regret your decision to come?' He shot her a look
that she felt was one of hope. No doubt he wanted her to
say that she regretted coming. He would probably be all
smiles and charm then. He might even offer to drive her
back to London in order to get rid of her quickly.

'No,' she stated firmly. 'I merely want to know as
much as possible. I wouldn't want to—to . . .'

'Put a foot wrong?' he enquired sardonically. 'Very
well, *señorita*. We advertised for someone with higher
qualifications with the hope that it might bring forth a
more stable, mature person. You are therefore a great
surprise, as you can imagine. I rather think that Señor
Bloom was overwhelmed by your appearance and that,
for the first time in his life, the dust left his veins and his
blood ran hot.'

'My qualifications are very good, Señor Conde,' Laura

snapped, confused and embarrassed by his pointed remarks. 'Mr Bloom is an old gentleman with impeccable manners.'

'And very good eyesight, no doubt,' he murmured, his eyes firmly on the road, his mind clearly dismissing the subject already.

'You haven't told me anything that I did not already know, Señor Conde. You've not told me about the Condesa, the times when I'll be free, the state of her health, her likes and dislikes . . .'

'My likes and dislikes are probably going to be your greatest worry, *señorita*,' he warned her softly. 'The Condesa is gentle and kind. I am not. As to my mother's health,' he added in a hard voice, 'I would have expected that Miguel Hernandes would have told you during your lengthy chat.'

'Oh, is that his name?' Laura said quickly, anxious to steer him away from the chat, not wanting to drag Doctor Hernandes into any kind of trouble.

'I am surprised that you do not know already,' he rejoined harshly. 'You seemed to take to each other like kindred spirits from the first sight. You were in there long enough to have planned a conspiracy of far-reaching effect!'

'We're members of the same profession, *señor*. It's surely natural that we should feel reasonably comfortable in each other's presence? Obviously I'm used to speaking to doctors, I've spent many years doing it.'

'And you are not used to speaking to dark, thunderous characters like me,' he finished for her, his face set and hard.

'I said nothing of the sort and meant nothing of the sort,' Laura answered hotly. 'I sincerely hope you will not let your dislike of Doctor Hernandes colour your relationship with me.'

His dark eyes slanted her a haughty glance.

'I assure you, *señorita*, I will allow nothing to colour my relationship with you. You already know my opinion of you, and it can be summed up in one word: unsuitable! As to Doctor Hernandes, what makes you imagine that I dislike him? I chose him especially to run the hospital. I cannot work with anyone that I dislike.'

'I—I'm sorry.' Laura looked away, confused and annoyed. 'You behaved as if you were angry.'

'I behave as I wish,' he remarked airily, the matter clearly closed, and Laura's own lips tightened. He certainly did! No wonder his mother had heart trouble, she thought sourly, she was likely to need nursing herself before her time at the castle was up. Only her stubborn nature and her determination to see a thing through to the end prevented her from telling him that she would not even bother to unpack, that he could get himself a nice 'substantial' nurse elsewhere.

'Your luggage will be at the *castillo* by the time we arrive,' he said in a more placatory tone after a while, but Laura was not in any way placated. Somehow, she was not now approaching her new job in a professional way. He had brought everything down to a personal level. He was irritating and confusing, and far too much of a man, she thought, glancing at his arrogant profile quickly and secretly. He had managed to cut the very ground away from her feet and nothing that he did or said was either expected or normal. Deep down, she knew that she could not cope with him and the knowledge was not welcome.

Upon their arrival at the castle he led her from the car, his hand firmly on her arm in what was probably a courteous gesture. Nevertheless, Laura felt like a mutinous child who had been found wandering and who was now being brought back firmly to be punished. Everything he did, no matter how slight, seemed to rob her of authority, and she silently admitted her mistake in coming here.

'Escort Sister Marsh to her room,' the Conde ordered as a plump, dark-haired girl appeared as if by magic, and even the words he used rang uneasily in Laura's ears. He might well have been saying that she was to be locked up again. 'You may also introduce yourself and tell the Sister of your own duties,' he added coldly.

'*Sí, señor.*' The girl didn't quite curtsy, but it was certainly implied and Laura took two deep breaths to control the surge of annoyance that rose inexplicably to the surface.

Why he should annoy her so much she couldn't understand. She really didn't care what he thought of her, she was quite sure of her own capabilities and he was at liberty to behave in any way he wished in his own castle. She already knew that he was a count, nobility, with ancestors stretching back to the days of the men who had wrested Spain from the hands of the Moors, but he had got under her skin and she was going to have a hard time treating him as an employer. She was going to have a hard time behaving rationally, even; she had a great desire now to turn and shake him, but he towered over her like a frightening illusion from the past.

The sight of her room, however, put all other thoughts from her mind. To say it was beautiful was an understatement. There was a tranquillity here that acted like a strong drug, and she felt her tight shoulders relax as a sigh of pleasure escaped her.

The room was steeped in luxury, the smooth white walls relieved here and there by the mellow stonework of the original building, great, towering panels of stone that stood out into the room and yet looked elegant and delicate because of the fine porcelain and silver ornaments set into the many alcoves that had been left in their towering height.

The walls were hung with beautiful pictures, gold framed and colourful, the carpet a soft green that gave the room a delightful femininity, and Laura was enchanted.

One wall was dominated by a hugh french window, now slightly open, letting in the soft evening breeze that blew the fine silk curtains, giving Laura a glimpse of delicately fashioned wrought iron at the edge of the balcony. The perfume of flowers came in tantalising waves across the whole room and her eyes met the smiling gaze of the maid.

'What a delightful room!'

'Sí, señorita. You were to have had another room at the far side of the castle, but the Conde rang from the hospital to say that you were to have this one instead. I have already pressed your clothes and hung them in the wardrobe.'

'You have? But why? I can do all that sort of thing for myself. It's very kind of you, but . . .'

'I am to be your maid, señorita. El Conde has ordered it, and I am honoured. I am also surprised. He does not like me.'

Suddenly, Laura found herself laughing, her natural good humour and exuberance rising above her misgivings.

'That makes two of us. I think the Conde doesn't like me either; but really, I don't need a maid. I'll speak to the Conde.' She couldn't reckon this up. She had been given a special room and a maid as if her stay here was to be prolonged, and yet, a short while ago, he had been anxious to see the back of her. Perhaps he had telephoned the Condesa while she had been with Doctor Hernandes. Perhaps the Condesa had told him to let her stay. The thought delighted her and removed some of her growing fears. Somebody then was capable of ordering the Conde about. It was a pleasant thought.

'Please, señorita, do not ask to be without a maid. The Conde will think that I have already displeased you and, as I seem to displease him every day, I will be relegated to the lower floors immediately.'

'I can't think what you could do for me—er . . .?'

'Maria, *señorita*. I can do everything for you—prepare your clothes, run your bath, many things that you will need. You are a nursing Sister from England and you will not be expected to do other things for yourself.'

There seemed to be nothing that she could do about it at present and Laura nodded her agreement, asking when she could see the Condesa. The plump little maid disappeared with a wide smile, promising to be back in no time at all with the news.

In a situation that she had never faced before, Laura went towards the balcony with a little sigh, wondering how some of the more senior Sisters would have coped with this.

She was young to be a Sister. Dedication and a natural flair for the job had earned her early promotion, but it was only during the last six months that she had risen from senior staff nurse to Sister. She realised that the Conde had expected a much older person and from his remarks she could only assume that he had wanted someone with the appearance of a wrestler, her ample bosom glittering with nursing medals. How would he have reacted to someone like that? she wondered. She knew plenty of Sisters like that who could have dealt with the Conde very adequately between breakfast and lunch, but she was beginning to doubt her own ability to deal with him.

She stood for a few minutes looking across at the gardens. The sun was sinking rapidly, but it was still possible to see the nearer scene. It was, like everything else here, beautiful. The toss of water from the fountains gladdened the eye and there were thick, clipped hedges, secret places where the paths led around pools and flower beds. The garden was laid out for peace and tranquillity.

It was elegant and enticing and she knew that it would be surrounded by high walls. This was a part of Spain that had been well loved by the Moors, a part they had relinquished with sorrow, and their walled gardens still stood in many of the places they had held, a haven of peace after endless wars. There was a silence, a beauty, almost a healing power, and she could well imagine the Condesa's reluctance to give up her hobby and delight.

With another sigh, she went into the luxurious bathroom, her hands touching the soft towels, the delicately perfumed soap. The warm peach and floral decoration of the tiles and fitments were a feast to the eye, and she tried hard to dismiss the Conde from her mind. She stripped off her clothes and stood under the warm shower, the water pouring a pleasurable cascade over her that brought a feeling of well-being to her body, and then she dressed in white jeans and soft, dark blue top, brushing her hair to a glittering shine and turning with a smile as Maria came back into the room.

'The Condesa will see you in the morning, *señorita*. She is resting now and the Conde stoppped me from going in to see her. He says that tomorrow will be quite soon enough. She was not well today,' she added mournfully. 'We are all glad that you are here. The Condesa is well loved in the *castillo*. She is a very gentle lady.'

'I'll do my best for her, Maria,' Laura said softly, and earned herself a brilliant smile. She didn't feel much like smiling herself, though. 'Tomorrow will be quite soon enough.' Soon enough no doubt to inflict her on his mother. No wonder she couldn't get him out of her mind; even here he intruded.

'You have a large bruise on your forehead, *señorita*,' Maria observed solemnly. 'We were sorry about your accident. The car has been taken into the village, but it may have to go to town. We heard that the radiator was smashed,' she added with pleasure, glorying in her technical knowledge, and Laura wondered if she always spoke using the royal plural or if she was the spokeswoman for the whole castle. She was bouncy and talkative. No wonder the Conde disliked her! She looked as if she might just answer back.

'I think I'll go into the garden, then,' Laura announced firmly, but Maria looked doubtful.

'The sun has almost set and the gardens are very extensive, *señorita*. It will be possible to lose yourself in the dark. I would come with you, but I think that the Señor would not like that. There are some parts of the garden where we may not go; they are private to the family.'

'Then I expect I will not be allowed to go there, either,' Laura said quietly, determined not to be seduced into the aristocratic ways of the Conde. 'I'll be all right, don't worry.'

'I could show you the side door if you like' Maria said anxiously. 'If you cross the great hall, the Conde will be almost sure to notice you, and he will also notice the great bruise on your head and he will be angry with me for not putting you straight to bed.'

'All right.' Laura couldn't help laughing at the idea of being put to bed like a child, and also at Maria's unlikely belief that the Conde would be concerned even if she were to be totally covered in bruises, but she didn't want Maria to be at the receiving end of the Conde's displeasure, so she allowed herself to be led down a dark and narrow staircase and she slipped out secretly into the dusk.

It was like a walk in paradise. The perfume of the flowers was almost too strong and the air was like balm on her skin. Laura took in great deep breaths of air, her head back and her eyes almost closed in pleasure. The very atmosphere made her feel sensuous, more of a woman than she had ever been, and her active

imagination peopled the silent gardens with tall, dark
Moors in their white robes, with soldiers in brightly
coloured swinging capes, with tall, dark, handsome
Spaniards.

She stopped that train of thought very quickly. The
tall, dark, handsome Spaniard in residence at the
moment was going to battle with her every day, and she
could well do without weaving him into her romantic
pictures.

The sound of water drew her to a courtyard and she
stood entranced by a splashing fountain, its crystal
waters just catching the few last rays of the dying sun. It
was so beautiful that she could not stop the contented
sigh that left her lips.

There was suddenly the rush of wings, the air
disturbed by the swooping power of some huge creature,
and Laura gave a little yelp of surprise and fear, covering
her head and running from the fountain straight into two
powerful arms that tightened momentarily around her.
When she raised scared eyes, she found herself looking
into the cool dark eyes of the Conde.

'Something has frightened you, Sister Marsh?' he
asked as if he expected that almost anything would.

'I—I was startled,' she confessed, struggling free from
the arms that still held her. 'Something swooped on me.'

'You appear to be undamaged,' he observed, his eyes
roaming coolly over her. 'Then, perhaps, a blue-eyed
inglesa could not be expected to have the courage of a
Spanish woman.'

'Women in England are not accustomed to having
dirty great bats with a wing span of twenty feet diving at
them, Señor Conde!' she snapped, her fear quite gone.

'A great exaggeration I think, *señorita*,' he returned
scathingly. 'The eagle owl that swept close to you is not a
dirty great bat, as you said so inelegantly. He is a very
beautiful creature with a wing span of five feet. He was

seeking his supper, and no doubt your silvery hair attracted him. It is true that he has a taste for the silver dove, but you are quite beyond his capabilities. Certainly if he had captured you, he would have been at great pains to return you the moment that you opened your mouth.'

'I'll go back into the castle,' Laura said firmly, taking a deep breath to control her temper.

The lights had come on in the lower rooms, lighting up the silver shine of her hair and leaving the Conde in greater shadow and she couldn't now see which was the garden door that Maria had shown her. She felt at a great disadvantage being unable to see what was gleaming in those dark, unfathomable eyes, and she took a rather hesitant step forward.

'I will show you the way, Sister Marsh,' he said with great relish. 'It is not a good idea to roam the grounds at night and for the time that you are here, you are, I suppose, under my care. I would not wish you to have a further accident and, who knows,' he added sarcastically, 'even now, the eagle owl may be in the forest gathering reinforcements.'

Laura didn't deign to answer. She couldn't bear him laughing, but she knew that he was.

Even in her annoyance, though, her eyes wandered over the now dark shape of the castle as it towered into the night sky, and the Conde came to a halt beside her.

'Impressive, is it not?' he enquired softly.

'It's unbelievable,' she confessed. 'So beautiful that it's just a little frightening.'

'You are unused to such grandeur, *señorita*?' He wasn't being sarcastic for once, and she looked across at him with a little laugh of surprise.

'I've never been in a castle before, Señor Conde, other than in old ruins. Few people have the good fortune to live in such splendour. It's hardly the norm.'

'Where did you live in England, before you took up

nursing? Where is your home?'

'I suppose I don't really have one,' she confessed. 'After my father died, I began to live in the nurses' home; there's one attached to most hospitals, or very close by.'

'And your mother?'

'She died when I was seven,' Laura told him quietly. 'My father and I were alone for a very long time. We were very close.'

'And yet you went to university, no doubt, and left him completely alone?'

She stiffened for a moment, wondering if he was prodding her into anger again, but he seemed to be merely interested and she let it go.

'No. I didn't go to university. I always wanted to be a nurse and I started training straight from school. I could live at home. It wasn't far away. Anyhow,' she added with a little smile, 'it could never have been afforded for me to go to university.'

'You resent that?' he asked, and she swung round in surprised annoyance. She should have known better than to chat normally with this cold, superior aristocrat.

'No, of course not! I doubt if I would have gone even if we could have afforded it. My father and I were quite alone in the world. We needed each other!'

'Yes,' he observed quietly. 'It is a shock for a child to lose its mother. Now, however, you are no longer alone, *señorita*. You have your—almost—fiancé. What is his name, this man? What does he do?'

'His name is David Elliott and he's a doctor,' she said briefly, still ruffled that she had been thought to resent her more lowly upbringing.

'A doctor? Yes, I can see that it would be natural. Women tend to marry the people that they work with or that they have been to school with. It is safer, no? More comfortable.'

'There should be more to marriage than safety and

comfort, in my opinion,' Laura said firmly, wondering uneasily how she had managed to get herself into this kind of conversation with the Conde. 'In any case, I haven't decided if I will marry David.'

Her tone was meant to bring the conversation to an end, but he had other ideas.

'You came here to get away from him? To make up your mind?' he enquired astutely, his voice hardening. 'I hope, Sister Marsh, that your distracted thoughts will not lessen your care for the Condesa!'

'I'm not distracted, Señor Conde! I'm very level-headed and efficient!'

'My mother needs more than efficiency, *señorita*. She needs care and kindness. She is gentle herself and can well do without either worry of seeing another's distress or receiving vague attention, however well meant.'

She opened her mouth to answer, feeling on the very edge of violence, but, to her astonishment, he smiled and held up his hand.

'However, as you assure me that you are not distracted, we need pursue the matter no further, as it is clear that you will think very little about this man if you are prepared to travel so far from him. It is obvious, too, that he does not love you or he would not have let you go. The matter can therefore be forgotten.

After one moment of open-mouthed astonishment at his cool intrusion into her private life, Laura erupted into anger.

'You know nothing about me that you haven't read in my application,' she stormed. 'You know nothing about my feelings, about my private life, about my hopes or dreams. You also know nothing about David! It's not in any case any of your business! You merely employ me, and I don't recall asking for your advice about my private life!'

'I may know nothing about your dreams and hopes,

señorita,' he agreed, staring at her angry face with raised
eyebrows, 'but I do know that you have a very wicked
little temper. Perhaps your doctor friend has discovered
this, too, and was glad to see you leave? Perhaps he is
even now sitting in tranquillity while you storm in Spain?
I can well see why he is only prepared to be almost your
fiancé! I begin to doubt whether or not you should even
be introduced to the Condesa. However, we will see. For
now, let us go inside before some feathery creature makes
the fatal mistake of attacking you.'

The Conde ignored the fact that she was shivering
with rage and she was led firmly and calmly around the
front of the castle, where he signalled her to precede him
through the heavy oaken doors that stood partly open.
He completely ignored her still bubbling rage and then,
as she stepped inside, she was stunned into silence and
immobility by her first glimpse of the place that was
obviously the great hall of which Maria had spoken.

The vast expanse of floor, bright with Andalusian tiles
that had weathered to warm, mellow colours with age,
the soaring height of the ceiling, the stark beauty of the
towering stone walls, took her breath away and left her
speechless.

One enormously long oak table of great age held the
centre of the floor, its sombre colour brightened by bowls
of flowers arranged in almost savage beauty down its
length. There were shields and swords on the walls, the
shields bearing the crest that she had seen carved into the
high stone arch that spanned the courtyard, and, rising
from the end of the hall, an imposing staircase that
looked large enough to take a whole company of soldiers.

At the top, the staircase split into two curving flights
that were lost in the shadows as they passed beyond the
reach of the illumination of the crystal chandeliers that
glittered in the hall.

'It is a shock, eh?' The Conde was watching the

changing expressions on her face and she turned to him wide-eyed, her anger forgotten in her utter awe at the place.

'How can I have missed it when you brought me in earlier?' she asked.

'You came in through the courtyard at the back. The hall there is less imposing, but also less alarming to the visitor.'

'I feel I should whisper or spin round looking at the place until I'm dizzy,' Laura said in a subdued voice.

'You have been made dizzy enough for one day, I think,' he said firmly. 'There is an interesting bruise on your forehead and I think that, for tonight, your dinner can be served in your room so that you can go to bed early. Tomorrow, you will dine with me and the others of our little domain.'

'Oh no, I don't think . . .' She knew it to be useless, even before her sentence petered out under the dark lash of his eyes.

'But I do think, *señorita*,' he corrected with hard determination. 'You will not eat in the kitchen; you will not hide in your room, unless you are ill. Do not be afraid,' he added drily, 'I will see that you do not use the wrong fork.'

'I'm quite capable of eating properly,' snapped Laura, the momentary magic of the great hall disappearing as her anger rose again. 'I naturally assumed that such a splendid castle would have an equally splendid dining room. As I came here to work, I think my clothes would not meet the standard required!'

'Then, if you stay, we shall have to do something about that, no?' the Conde murmured softly, his eyes glittering down at her like the sparkle of sunlight on jet. 'Anything that troubles you can be taken care of easily. You are simply required to use your skill and kindness to assist the Condesa and to be reasonably obedient.'

'Obedience does not come readily to me, Señor Conde!' Laura retorted hotly, realising that any pleasantness on his part was merely a momentary lapse and that she might as well continue the battle, but he did not rise to the bait. Instead, he took her firmly by the arm and took her to one of the many doors that flanked the great hall.

'Your disobedience can also be taken care of easily,' he warned darkly. 'But for now, come, let us allay your fears. The dining room!'

He opened the door with a flourish and flicked a switch. Instantly, the room was flooded with light from three huge chandeliers, and Laura's heart sank like a stone at what looked more like a state banqueting hall than a family dining room.

Everything was on a massive scale, from the gleaming silver on the dark, heavy sideboards to the long sombre dining-table that would surely seat fifty or sixty guests, the great damask-covered chairs arranged in orderly display along its length like so many thrones.

'This, as you see, is the dining room,' said the Conde, his eyes appraising her dismayed face with sardonic amusement. 'However, this is where we eat.'

He flung open an adjoining door and a breath of reality returned as a beautiful and comfortable room, softly lit, the table already laid for dinner, sprang into view.

'We like to be comfortable. We do not use the more noble dining room unless necessity forces it upon us. I imagine that here you will be able to cope with the situation. Your clothes are no problem, and as to the choice of the correct fork, watch me, I will signal you in plenty of time.'

'Why are you so insulting and unpleasant to me?' Laura demanded angrily, turning to face him with fire openly in her eyes, infuriated further when she saw laughter at the back of his dark eyes.

He tilted her rebellious face with one strong brown hand, his dark eyes searching her expression.

'Perhaps you bring out the devil in me,' he suggested with amusement. 'Perhaps it is your profession and my desire to point out to you your many inadequacies, or perhaps I simply like to test the extent of the fire in you.'

He released her and pulled on a brocade sash that hung by the door and, almost at once, Maria appeared, like a dark-haired jack-in-the-box, to stand uneasily in the open doorway, listening intently to the rapid flow of Spanish that the Conde almost hurled at her.

'*Si, Señor Conde*,' she said, her head nodding vigorously as she memorised his orders.

'Maria will see that you get safely to your room, *señorita*. She will also deal with your nasty bruise.'

'I can . . .' Laura's retort died in her throat as he took her hand and raised it to his lips.

'I'm quite sure that you can,' he remarked soothingly and obscurely. '*Hasta mañana, señorita*.'

He turned to the hall and walked off. He had given his instructions. There was nothing further to be said and his interest in the situation had disappeared. His broad shoulders and his easy walk said it all, and Laura was left wondering how she was going to be able to get the better of this disturbing, unpredictable man. She could still feel the hard warmth of his hand on her skin, and a soft blush ran over her face as she realised that it had given her a quick thrill of pleasure.

CHAPTER THREE

THE next morning Laura was up in good time, fully recovered from her accident and intent upon bringing normality back into her life. The Conde was a man who needed to be kept at arm's length—or further—and today she intended to be firmly in her role of Sister Marsh before he could pounce on her in his devastating way and undermine her grip on reality.

She looked at her reflection in the mirror with grim satisfaction. The midnight blue of her slightly starched uniform dress contrasted sharply with the stiff white cuffs that ended the short sleeves. Her hair was swept up from its normal shoulder-length glory to pile high on her head above her slender neck, and she gave the starched white cap that topped it a final twist to enhance its crisp disciplined angle.

Sister Marsh, the terror of the wards! She grinned at her reflection in the mirror as she remembered Maria's awe-stricken glance at her when she had come to collect the breakfast tray and found the vulnerable *señorita* of the night before standing slim and straight-backed, buckling her dark belt around her small waist, her face cool and professional.

There would be no nonsense from his lordship today! She strode from the room in her dark low-heeled shoes and marched towards the stairs, upright and calm-faced, secure in her normal role.

Her heart gave a very unprofessional leap however, when, almost at the bottom of the grand staircase, she looked up and found the Conde waiting at the bottom of the steps, his strong legs apart, his hands on his hips and

46

murder in his flashing dark eyes.

'What do you imagine you are wearing?' he ground out angrily.

'Today is my first day on duty. Naturally I'm in uniform. If you could get someone to show me where the Condesa has her private rooms ...'

He glared with fury into her cool face.

'And have her scared out of her mind by the sight of you in your starched efficiency? You are here to be her *compañera*, to use your undoubted skills in any crisis of her health. You are not required to precipitate a crisis by appearing in rigid formality, your hair scraped underneath a stiff white cap that would probably slice off a man's fingers!'

'It's my normal uniform,' Laura said coldly, gleeful that she had for once got the upper hand.

'What is normal in an uncomfortable London hospital is not normal in my *castillo*!' he thundered. 'I can only conclude that you are either too heartless to be allowed anywhere near my mother or that you have retreated behind your cardboard-stiff fortress to prove to me that there is antiseptic liquid in your veins where normal women have warm blood. Change your clothes at once!'

'I'll do nothing of the kind!'

She stood small and defiant, looking down into his dark glittering eyes, and with a low growl he took a step towards her.

'You have one minute. After that, I do it myself!'

'You wouldn't dare!' Her calm manner was slipping rapidly as she determinedly held her ground.

'I would dare anything that I considered to be necessary, *señorita*. Changing you back into a woman would be an attractive occupation that would take very little time. You are wasting the minute.' He moved closer and Laura's nerve almost snapped. She was saved, however, by the appearance of a tall slim woman who came into the great hall from a room to one side of the stairs.

'Rodrigo darling, you sound like a storm over the mountains,' she said in a soft amused voice. 'Whatever is it that is causing you so much annoyance?'

The Condesa. Laura had no doubts. There seemed to be no resemblance between the Conde's dark, disturbing good looks and the slim, pale beauty of the woman who took his arm, but she had a grace and a bearing that spoke of years of wealth and authority, and the tranquillity of years of love, Laura added to herself as the Conde drew his mother's hand through his arm, his strong brown hand covering her fragile fingers.

'Oh!' She looked up and saw Laura and her face relaxed into a wider smile. 'Sister Marsh. I never expected to be lucky enough to have someone so beautiful in answer to the advertisement.'

'The Condesa de las Montanas, Sister Marsh,' the Conde said stiffly, his eyes flashing dangerously at Laura, his hand still protectively on his mother's, his whole demeanour one of tightly controlled anger.

'Come along, Sister Marsh,' the Condesa said happily, moving away from the protective arm of her son and motioning Laura to the open doorway. 'How very exciting this all is! Let's go back into my apartments.'

'*Madrecita!*' The Conde's anxious and warning note had the Condesa swinging round in surprise.

'It's quite all right, Rodrigo. What are you so worried about? Sister Marsh and I are quite capable of sorting everything out. I'm dying to talk to her.'

The dark eyes of Rodrigo Estéban Diaz, Conde de las Montanas, met the brilliant blue eyes of Sister Laura Marsh and she raised her eyebrows coolly, longing to burst into peals of laughter when his eyes narrowed to glittering dark slits and his mouth tightened to one hard straight line. He would accept defeat at the hands of his mother, but from no one else; he was a true Spaniard, and his dark glance told her that there would be retribution at the appropriate time.

The room that she entered was almost breathtakingly beautiful. The high ceiling, arched and domed as if it was yet another part of the older building that had been standing for so many generations, was white with gold tracery at its highest points.

Tall windows looked on to the gardens that were so dear to the Condesa, and the furniture in the room was lavish beyond Laura's wildest imaginings.

She was so enthralled by the splendour of the room that she turned, startled, as a ripple of laughter from the Condesa drew her attention to the far side of the room where the Condesa stood beside an exquisitely fashioned writing desk.

'You remind me so much of myself when I first came to the *castillo*. I was open-mouthed for months. Felipe was constantly sending out servants to find me when I lost myself in some corner of the castle or the grounds. You should be easy to find, though, with that exquisite hair. Rodrigo described you to me last night, and he certainly didn't do you justice. He seemed to think that I wouldn't want you here. He said you were not in any way like a nurse. How wrong he was!' She smiled, looking Laura up and down. 'You're so smart and efficient. Perhaps the way he found you coloured his judgment? How are you by the way?'

'I'm fine today,' Laura said quickly. 'It's how you are that's the question.'

So the Conde had decided that his mother would not want her here. Well, his mother clearly had a mind of her own and couldn't be pushed into having thoughts that were not her own either.

She was going to have difficulty keeping up her stiff image with this charming and delicate woman, though.

Her beauty and her ready laughter were too attractive to
be pushed aside and ignored. It would be harder to be a
nurse to the Condesa than to be a companion. It would be
hard to be a nurse in the splendour and beauty of the
castle, too, to say nothing of the disturbing influence of
the Conde. The whole place was ensnaring her.

'I'd better know what régime you're on,' she said
quickly. 'I didn't get the chance to ask Doctor Hernandes
about it.'

'Of course, you met Miguel. He's very nice, don't you
think? I expect you'll be seeing a lot of him—he haunts
the place. Between Rodrigo and Miguel, I sometimes feel
really backed into a corner; either one or the other seems
to be watching me constantly. I was rather hoping for an
ally in you.'

'You have one,' Laura said gladly, her face lighting up
with pure devilment. 'Two men have no chance
whatever against two women.'

'What a relief! Look at my tablets if you want to and
then let's go out into the gardens. I can't do what I used to
do out there, but I so enjoy being among the flowers. I
sometimes feel they'll die of neglect if I'm not seeing to
them personally, although the gardeners are really good,
but Rodrigo will never let them come in nowadays to
consult me, and there are so many little things that
irritate.'

After half an hour of walking slowly in the scented
magic of the gardens, moving behind the clipped secrecy
of tall hedges, looking into fountains and pools, Laura
felt relaxed and very much at home, only the Conde a
constant nagging worry at the back of her mind.

At one time, the Condesa had tucked her arm through
Laura's as they stood and watched the flash and glitter of
goldfish in a pool where lilies floated on the clear surface
and she had never removed her hand.

Something drew Laura's gaze to one of the upper

windows, and she was startled and a little alarmed to see the Conde looking down at them, his dark eyes unreadable, his face still. Clearly he was taking no chances that she would upset his mother. He was spying on them both and, rather than this annoying her, it brought a quick and unwelcome thrill of fear. He looked like someone from the past, standing there so still and silent, as if she had suddenly looked up and seen a ghost. She realised belatedly that he was looking straight into her wide and rather scared eyes and she looked away abruptly, a furtive glance seconds later showing her that he had gone.

'I really wish I could still garden,' the Condesa said wistfully later. 'I can't do anything about these little things that are not quite right, although sometimes I sneak out and do a bit of work. I suppose you think I'm fussy?'

'No, I understand really. My father loved his little garden and had much the same feelings that you have whenever he was unwell and had to be still. What about a compromise? I'll do the gardening and you sit and tell me what you want doing.'

'But you're a nurse, a hospital Sister!' the Condesa said, with all the awe of Maria in spite of her title and authority.

'I rather hoped I would end up by being just a friend,' Laura said softly. 'And my name is Laura. Please don't continue to call me Sister Marsh.' She had given in. The Condesa was delightful and some inner knowledge told her that the Conde would get his own way, whatever it was. Battling with him would have to be a little more subtle than the head-on attacks that she had attempted to beat him with so far; he was too strong and unsettling for that.

'Oh, what a dear girl you're going to be!' The Condesa's face lit up with smiles. 'Can you garden?'

'No, but you're going to teach me,' Laura said firmly.
'Now sit right there on that bench and don't move. I'll get
into the old gardening gear.'

The happy sound of the Condesa's laughter followed
her and lingered in her mind as she went quickly through
the great hall and up to her room. Old blue jeans that she
had considered discarding but had been reluctant to part
with soon took the place of her crisp uniform. A bright
red shirt that she had hung on to for years topped it off
and she slid her feet into comfortable sandals. Her long
hair, released from the formality of the confining pins
and starched cap, was combed into a long ponytail
behind her head, and she burst eagerly from her room,
bumping straight into the Conde as he strode silently
past her door.

'Oh! I—I'm sorry.' She stood looking up at him, his
expression halting her further progress.

'You are probably the most astonishing person I have
ever met,' he observed, his eyes roaming over her. 'You
left me earlier in the starched security of your uniform,
your face calm and cold, and now you appear like a
rocket, rushing eagerly from your room like an excited
child on her way to a trip to the sea.'

'I'm going to dig in the garden,' Laura said with what
she thought was a firmness to stop any counteracting
orders, but somehow it came out breathlessly under the
penetrating stare of his eyes.

'Really? Not in any haphazard fashion, I hope, like a
dog seeking his bone, or I will have some placating to do
with the gardeners.'

'The Condesa is fretting about little things that she
can't do and I offered to do them while she sits and
directs me. She shouldn't have anything to agitate her,'
she added, looking up into the cool surprise of his face,
her expression begging him not to interfere. She knew for
certain that what she was about to do would be good for

the Condesa, would lessen the strain, and that he could put a stop to it with one harsh word, one unthinking order.

'I have been watching you with my mother,' he said quietly. 'I owe you an apology for my unkind remarks and for my very bad temper. Perhaps you are not as fierce as you appear to be, perhaps I bring out the worst in you, or perhaps it is the great difference in our cultures. My mother at any rate looks calm and happy. I hope you will stay here with us.'

He was standing perfectly still, watching her intently, and she didn't know quite what to do or say. It would perhaps have been a good idea to say thank you, smile nicely and race off downstairs, but she wanted to make a dignified exit and somehow she couldn't think of one. And, also, she suddenly felt compelled to just go on looking at him as if he were ordering it, until the whole world seemed to shrink and there was only his face, only the dark, disturbing intensity of his eyes.

When his hand came slowly out to slide beneath her hair and cup the warmth of her nape as he drew her forward she went like someone in a dream, utterly fatalistic as his firm lips covered hers in a deep searching kiss.

'Why did you do that?' she whispered when at last he raised his head and looked at her searchingly.

'My thanks, of course,' he remarked softly, his eyes holding hers, 'and also the desire to know what it would be like to kiss a very small and fiery *inglesa* with hair like moonlight.' His hands came strong and sure to grip her shoulders. 'As an experiment it was a great success, well worth repeating.'

His mouth captured hers again before she could take more than a startled breath and, this time, his lips lingered in sensual exploration, almost as if he were searching her mind, kissing her in a way that she had never been kissed before as his arms tightened round her, making escape impossible.

Not that she was trying to escape, one part of her mind told her in disgust, but the rest of her mind accepted the enchanting magical feeling that flooded into it and swept through her body until the hands that had been plucking frantically at his shirt quietened like contented birds and lay softly against the power of his chest.

With no further need to hold her captive, his grip relaxed and his hands moved seductively over her back, moved to stroke her shoulder and the velvet smooth skin of her neck as the kiss went on endlessly. Until she seemed to have no memory left of anything but the hard power of his body, the warm excitement of his searching lips.

She swayed dizzily when at last he released her, unable it seemed to return to reality, still lost in some long-forgotten time like a faintly recalled dream, and his hands came to her shoulders again to steady her as she opened dazed eyes to find herself looking into a face alien and satisfied. His dark burning eyes seemed to belong to a man from some past generation and there was more of the Crescent than the Cross in the faint smile that curved his perfect but faintly cruel mouth.

'You are afraid of me,' he observed without any apparent satisfaction, 'but it does not matter. Run along and rejoin my mother. You have my permission to dig as many holes in the garden as your heart desires. If the gardeners complain, I will plant them in the holes up to their necks.'

He stroked one long hand down her pale face and then strode off, apparently totally unmoved by what had been to Laura the most devastating experience of her life. She still stood there in the darkened corridor, her hand to her mouth, her heart hammering, startled to find that she was making little whimpering sounds that were the

outward signs of her inner agitation, horrified by the
great surge of sexual excitement that had torn through
her as he held her.

It took a great deal of self-control to rejoin the
Condesa. She felt sure that her experience with the
Conde would show clearly on her face and, in retrospect,
it annoyed her immensely. He had called it an
experiment and clearly that was what it was. Unless it
was another ploy.

Could it be that the Conde, having suffered defeat in
trying to get rid of her originally, had now decided to
side-track his mother in a new way? It was a good way to
subdue any woman, a totally masculine way, a way that
would be typical of a man like the Conde de las
Montanas.

She flushed hotly as she recalled her reaction to him;
he could hardly have failed to notice. The whole thing
was bordering on madness, some gigantic, insane chess
game. She tightened her lips and bent to her task with
fury beginning to mount slowly inside her.

But even after a long time spent clearing up the little
areas of garden under the Condesa's window that were
slightly less than perfect, Laura still trembled inside with
the terrible shock of the sexual attraction that the Conde
held for her.

She had just finished, having been warned by the
Condesa that she was using muscles that she had not used
since she had crouched down as a child helping her father
in the small garden at home, when a tall, dark-haired
man sauntered along the path and stood smiling at the
picture they made.

'Eduardo, my dear!' The Condesa reacted with
pleasure as he bent to kiss her hand. 'Look at my nurse.
Isn't she delightful?'

'Unusual, certainly,' he said, bowing to Laura and
welcoming her with a smile.

'It's Laura's prescription for therapy,' the Condesa explained. 'She's decided to do the things that I can't, things that irritate me when they're left. I feel better already. I'm sure I'll be fine now—until Carlota Martinez arrives for dinner! And don't look like that,' she added as he shot her an amused but warning glance. 'Rodrigo knows I dislike her.'

He shrugged his shoulders with Latin eloquence and turned to Laura.

'I am Eduardo Calveros. Sister Marsh, is it not?'

'Oh, I'm sorry, Laura, I quite forgot to introduce you,' the Condesa said with the ease of someone who knows that all crimes will be forgiven her. 'Eduardo is the estate manager and Rodrigo's friend. He's been in Córdoba for a week and we've really missed him.'

'Thank you, Condesa Helen. I have missed you too. I wished to be here to protect you from the terrifying Sister you were expecting.' The smile he gave to Laura took all the sting from his words and the Condesa's ready laughter bubbled to the surface.

'She was all nurse earlier this morning, in a beautifully starched uniform, but I think she is no more conventional than I am. I've found her out. She battles with Rodrigo too. I discovered that earlier this morning too.'

'You were very busy earlier, it seems,' Eduardo observed with an indulgent smile. 'And you survived a battle with Rodrigo, *señorita*? *Muy bien!* He can rage like a fighting bull at the *corrida*.'

Laura found herself blushing and hoping that the Conde was miles away. She had not survived nearly so well in the soft darkness of the corridor, and the memory of it still made her heart race.

A further step on the terrace had the Condesa rising and holding out her hand as Doctor Hernandes appeared.

'So many visitors!' she exclaimed in pleased tones.

'Come, we will all go into my apartment and have coffee. Go ahead and ring the bell for my maid, Eduardo.'

'They said that you were here. I thought to catch you up to your tricks again, Condesa,' Doctor Hernandes confessed with the air of a man who is always welcome and knows it. 'I also hoped to have a chat with your—nurse.' His eyebrows rose in amusement as he noticed Laura in her jeans and red shirt.

'She was all the Sister Marsh you hoped for earlier', the Condesa explained, 'but I prefer her as she is, so no harsh words, Miguel. Come along.' She took his arm and led the way into her apartment, Laura following, wondering how she could continue to fit into the new role she had somehow adopted.

But it was easy to talk to all of them. She sat on a settee of oyster-coloured damask, talking to Eduardo Calveros as the Condesa dispensed coffee. He was a man of about the Conde's age, thirty-seven or eight, she supposed, but there the likeness ended. His good looks were gentle and, though his eyes flashed from time to time in true Latin fashion, he was as different from the Conde as to be another nationality.

They all were, and she realised that the Conde de las Montanas was a man alone, his heritage deep in his veins, his looks and nature rooted in the distant past, his modern veneer thinly disguising a spirit that would have been more at ease on horseback, sword in hand, wading through the waves that broke on the shores of some coastline of the Americas in the long-dead past, his men beside him, the banner of Spain plunged deep into the sand to claim the land for all time.

He belonged to the time of Cortés. His spirit was still the same as his ancestors who had helped to claim so much of the New World for their king. He was right when he had so astutely said he frightened her. She wondered if he was lonely, if he felt like an alien,

marooned on a distant planet where the distance was
time instead of miles of space.

'What do you do here, Señor Calveros?' she asked,
desperately forcing the distressing pictures that had
come to her mind well out of the way.

'I manage the nearer estates. This one and three others
within the province, although the estate that surrounds
the *castillo* is by far the largest and takes up most of my
time. I travel quite a bit too, though not so much as
Rodrigo. There are so many business interests that the
family have acquired over the centuries that he has to
work very hard. He flies all over the world.' He frowned.
'Sometimes I think that he does not like it too much
either. He is happier here riding Diablo through the
forest and keeping an eye on the activities of Condesa
Helen. She is often in poor health, but she is as wilful as
she was in her youth.'

'You knew her then?' Laura could not keep the
surprise from her voice, and he laughed openly.

'*Sí!* I live here! I grew up with Rodrigo. My father was
manager to Rodrigo's father, and when he died, I took
over. The Conde de las Montanas and I were reared
almost like brothers, despite his noble heritage and my
lowly beginnings. In Spain there is less of the master and
man syndrome than you would imagine, Sister Marsh.
Here we are all *hombres.*'

'I didn't mean that at all,' said Laura, embarrassed.
'And please call me Laura.'

'I know that you did not, Laura, and I think you will
soon be well liked in the Castillo del Fuego,' he added,
glancing at the Condesa. 'She looks better already and we
all adore her. Rodrigo will soon have no further excuse
for lingering on the estate. He will be more relaxed now
that you are here and soon he will be off on his travels
because, even though I suspect that he hates leaving the
estate, duty is strong within him and he will do anything

that duty demands, no matter how distressing to himself.'

'Come over here, Eduardo, and tell me about Córdoba,' the Condesa called, catching his glance in her direction. 'Miguel wishes to discuss me with my nurse in low professional whispers, do you not, Miguel?'

'Indeed I do,' he laughed, coming to sit beside Laura as Eduardo went with willing obedience to the Condesa's side.

'You have improved her already,' he said, smiling down at Laura. 'She is greatly at her ease, but do not relax your vigilance, and should you ever cease your battles with the Conde, mention the operation.' He looked worried and she nodded.

'I will, if the day ever arrives when I can see him for longer than a minute and not get annoyed.'

'I know,' he laughed ruefully. 'We are in the same boat, you and I. We will stand back to back against attack, although I have little hope of success when a whole team of consultants have tackled him and been dusted off soundly. He is too formidable for normal mortals.'

The formidable man in question chose that moment to appear, and Laura realised with dismay that her heart had started to leap every time she saw him.

'I see that you are entertaining visitors,' he observed, smiling at the Condesa and glancing with cold, watchful eyes at Miguel Hernandes and Laura sitting in quiet conspiracy on the settee. 'You are back, I see, Eduardo. I should have known you would hurry to see my mother before you reported to me.'

'She is more beautiful than you, *amigo*,' Eduardo retorted with a grin that the Conde returned easily. Laura watched surreptitiously as he seated himself close to Eduardo and the Condesa, ignoring Doctor Hernandes except for a brief nod, his eyes passing over Laura as if she was not there.

She was startled by the burst of disappointment that

she felt. It seemed that she had been right after all and she talked more readily to the doctor, adopting the Conde's cool attitude, behaving herself as if the meeting in the corridor had not occurred and concentrating all her attention on Miguel Hernandes. It was only later that she glanced up to find that the Conde had left as silently as he had appeared, never speaking to her at all, never even acknowledging her presence.

What she had expected she could not imagine. He was behaving exactly as she had thought. If he was different from his own people, he was light years away from her, and in any case, she told herself firmly, she didn't even like him. There was just this alarming sexual attraction, and for his part she was certain now that he had decided to make life too uncomfortable and embarrassing for her to wish to stay. It was unforgivable!

It was later, in the evening when she was wandering in the grounds, that she thought with misgivings about dinner. The Conde had ordered her appearance yesterday and the Condesa had taken it for granted that she would have Laura's company and support, confessing that without that support she would probably have feigned tiredness in order to have escaped the meal herself.

'I hate doing that,' she had confided to Laura. 'It worries Rodrigo, but I cannot bear the Señorita Martinez, and she will be here in good time for the meal, as I have reason to know from her past record.

'You shouldn't have things to agitate you,' Laura had said with annoyance, her professional opinion rising above etiquette.

'I know,' the Condesa had sighed, 'but I think Rodrigo is too taken with the woman to realise quite how much I dislike her. He is, after all, thirty-eight already and hasn't shown the slightest inclination to marry. Carlota Martinez is probably the nearest thing to a regular attraction that I've observed. He must marry, of course, but if he chooses her, then I really think my time at the Castillo del Fuego is over. I can't foresee the time when I would be prepared to face her every day. For tonight, however, I have you and Eduardo, and I've also invited Miguel Hernandes. You see, I'm cunning,' she had laughed. 'I've built up a buffer against the Señorita Carlota. You will support me, Laura dear?'

She couldn't refuse, but as she walked in the grounds now, Laura found herself wondering who this *señorita* was who had captured the Conde's heart and how he had dared to behave as he had done in the quiet darkness of the corridor when he was planning to marry some unsuspecting female, probably in the very near future. Her opinion of him dropped rapidly and her anger at herself rose in proportion.

It did not, however, prevent the now expected leap of her heart when she found him walking slowly towards her in the fading sunlight.

'Ah, Maria told me that you were out here now that your busy day is over. Come, I want to show you something.' He took her arm and turned her smartly round, marching her along as if nothing but smiles and kind words had ever been between them, as if he had not ignored her this morning in the Condesa's suite. He had been closeted with Eduardo since then and she could see he was tired, but she refused to be anything but formal with him.

'I really must go inside, Señor Conde,' she remarked stiffly. But he propelled her along with more speed than gentleness.

'Soon,' he said softly. 'First there is something that you should see. I promise that it will intrigue you.'

As he clearly intended to have his own way as usual, and as her only means of escape was to have an undignified struggle with him, Laura allowed herself to be led around the clipped hedges and out into an open part of the gardens where there was a splendid view of the front of the castle.

'Good. We arrive in time. Stand here and watch the walls.' She turned dutifully. It was a pleasure to look at the castle and, though she had not the faintest idea of what she should be looking for, Laura stood and watched, her annoyance receding as the tranquillity of the place took a grip on her mind and heart.

Suddenly her interest quickened as she saw a flash of fire ripple over the mellow walls.

'Oh!' She turned to Rodrigo, and as quickly turned back when she found him watching her with disturbing intensity.

'Continue to watch,' he advised quietly. 'It has not yet really begun and it does not last too long.'

The almost secret flash came again, and then the whole spectacle of the fires of the *castillo* unfolded and came alive before Laura's entranced gaze. Flames of orange, red and gold mixed with vivid blues and purples, greens and flares of silver seemed to set the walls of the castle ablaze with light, and Laura realised why this beautiful place was called the Castle of Fire.

She stood in silent awe as the coloured flames played over the walls of the castle that faced the highest peak of the mountain. It seemed that the whole of the castle must go up in flames as she watched. It was like a wall of flame that had been sprinkled with salt to bring out every colour of the spectrum and the whole spectacle was conducted in silence all the more awesome because the crackle of a real fire and the fear that it would bring were totally absent.

'What is it?' She never looked away as she whispered the words.

'It is the dying sun.' The Conde's voice was almost in her ear as he replied. 'Many times the castle has been under attack because of the fires. In the olden days, they used to think that my ancestors had brought back jewels from their adventurous trips to the countries of South America. They imagined that the fires came from the glitter of the jewels embedded in the walls of the castle. If you look carefully and closely you can still see the holes and scratches that these people made on the castle walls in their attempts to take away the jewels that were in fact only there in their imagination.'

'Then what causes the glitter and the flames?' Laura never turned, even now; it was too wonderful to look away from, too enthralling to miss even a second. The utter silence of the gardens and the brilliant display of the fires left her speechless, almost, lost in the wonder of it all, and there was a strange satisfaction in the Conde's voice when he answered.

'When the castle was first built, either by accident or design, no one knows, small pieces of glittering rock were embedded in the walls. It was perhaps some fanciful idea of one of my ancestors, but whatever the reason, I think the results would have been a great surprise to the builders because these worthless stones come to life as the sun sets over the mountain peaks. We are given this display which is like the aurora that can be seen in the northern countries. Here, it is captured for ever on the walls of my castle until the sun dips beyond the highest peak of the mountains.'

'It's beautiful!' Laura was so entranced that even his nearness was simply right and comforting as together they watched the fiery display.

After many minutes, as they stood together in silence, the colours seemed to lose some of their strength and, saying that the sun was setting, the Conde put his hand firmly on her arm and turned her away.

'Oh, can't we stay to see the fires die?'

'No!' A harshness returned to his voice that had been

absent since he had confronted her in the grounds. 'You have things to do, I'm sure!'

'I've finished for the day! Do you expect me to work all day and all night?' She turned on him angrily, annoyed at the implication that she was standing around, wasting the time he was paying for when it had been he who had insisted that she came out here.

'You have to dress for dinner at any rate,' he said coolly, propelling her towards the castle and allowing for no lingering. 'As you have as yet nothing suitable to wear it will no doubt take some time and great deal of thought to get ready to dine with me.'

His insolence would have taken her breath away, even if his rapid progress towards the castle had not been doing that already, and she had no chance to speak until he had ushered her into the great hall with unseemly haste and closed the door with a resounding bang.

She spun round and faced him then like a small silver-haired fury, her hands clenched, her body trembling with anger under the towering grandeur of the massive stone walls.

'You, Señor Conde, are the most annoying, the most unpleasant man it's ever been my misfortune to meet!'

'All because I refused to let you see the fires die, *señorita*?' he enquired with raised eyebrows. 'That is surely a harsh and overstated opinion.'

'It is my opinion nevertheless, *señor*. You're impossible, arrogant, unkind and insensitive. I may be only an employee in your splendid castle, but I'm not accustomed to being treated as you've treated me!'

'So!' he murmured dangerously, 'you have decided on the role that you will assume? Perhaps you would like to leave your beautiful room and be relegated to one of the turrets where you undoubtedly imagine that the other old family retainers sleep? You no doubt also imagine that I hold feudal sway over the surrounding countryside, taking a share in the profits of the hardworking peasants! It will undoubtedly have crossed your rebellious little mind that I almost certainly claim the *droit de seigneur* with the young maidens in the *pueblos*!'

'I shouldn't be at all surprised,' Laura snapped, turning away. 'You're completely unfeeling!'

His hands shot out and before she could move she was hauled against him, his hand on her hip, his other behind her neck under the heavy fall of her hair.

'Whatever else I am, *señorita*,' he rasped, 'I am not unfeeling, not when I have my hands on you!' His lips captured hers and she felt for one panicky second that she was being savaged. There was no sensuality, no tenderness, none of the gentle questing movement that he had shown before when he kissed her. This was a punishment for speaking to him as an equal, and she struggled under the relentless pressure of his hands.

Only when her struggles ceased did he release her, to stand looking down at her with angry eyes, his strong lean body so tense that she dared not make a move. She felt she was facing a tiger who would spring at her if she so much as blinked an eyelid.

'*Bueno!*' he growled, his breathing still harsh and heavy. 'Know what to expect if you cross me again, you sharp-tongued little dragon!'

'I don't have to put up with this kind of treatment!' Laura gasped as soon as her unsteady breathing would allow, painfully aware that they were standing in the great hall where at any moment some passing servant might see them, although the Conde seemed to care not at all. 'I shall pack my cases and return to England tomorrow!'

'You have a contract!' the Conde reminded her angrily.

'Breaking my contract with you will cause me no concern whatever,' she pronounced, his cool arrogance causing her temper to rise over the unsteady beating of her heart. 'I made no use of the air ticket you offered. I came here under my own steam and at my own expense.'

'And I rescued you!' he grated, fury in his eyes. 'Your own steam was rather inadequate, I think, when you had to be released from your car and carted off to hospital.'

'You may put that down to experience, Señor Conde,' Laura advised him sharply. 'Tomorrow I shall leave and stay in a hotel until my car is repaired. Don't worry, I'll pay for the repairs myself. It will be well worth it to get away from you!'

'And of course, you are quite prepared to desert my mother who has already placed her trust in you. Do you normally desert your patients, Sister Marsh?'

'No, but then I'm not normally subjected to abuse and physical assault by their relatives,' she rejoined tartly.

'Physical assault? You think it was that?' he asked in a quiet voice that should have warned her but did not. 'Then I must correct the error.'

Still within reach, she was powerless to flee from the strong arms that lashed her to him as, mindless of the open aspect of the great hall, careless as to who might see them, he kissed her into silence, this time with no cruelty, in no way punishing, but with a slow enjoyment that set her pulses racing and had her clenching her fists to keep her hands from exploring the thickness of his black hair.

'You are willing enough in my arms,' he murmured softly, looking down into the wide blue eyes that could do nothing but stare at him. 'Do you feel like this when your doctor friend kisses you? I ask myself, and I think not. If you did, you would be still in England, eagerly planning your wedding and looking forward to your wedding night.'

He released her as they both heard the sound of a car that ground to a halt outside the heavy doors, and as he moved to open the doors, Laura fled on trembling legs.

'Ah, Carlota! How are you?'

'Well, darling, now that I see you.'

Laura turned quickly from her position halfway up the stairs in time to see the Conde with another woman in his arms, his lips kissing her as he had just kissed Laura, and, to her horror, she felt a burst of feeling that was frighteningly akin to jealousy.

Of course, Señorita Martinez. What a pity she had not arrived silently a few minutes earlier!

Laura fled to her room and straight into the bathroom to hide from the sharp eyes of Maria. She was filled with outrage, still trembling and, disgracefully, still excited.

'He thinks he's too clever for you, my girl,' she told herself sternly in the mirror. 'He's found a very good way of unsettling you. Try giving him a good hard slap on his noble face!'

She couldn't think why she had not done that already, although the thought of the Conde's reaction really frightened her. He was capable of ferocity when she used only words against him; a slap would probably bring on her early demise, and, she added to herself thoughtfully, her immediate dismissal. Oh, the cunning, cruel man!

CHAPTER FOUR

FACING them all at dinner would be an ordeal, Laura knew that, and all she could do was prepare carefully. Had there only been the Conde involved, she would have refused to dine with him, going hungry rather than sit at the same table. But she had allowed the Condesa to think that she would be there, an extra support when the woman the Condesa disliked would be at the table. She had to appear, and she could only be thankful that Miguel Hernandes would also be present.

She had few clothes with her for such an occasion. She had never expected to be dining with the Conde and his mother; in fact she had given little thought to it. She came from an ordinary family, and what would be expected of her tonight she had no idea.

With Maria's help, however, she selected a dress of pale turquoise, relying on its simplicity to cover for its faults. Not that it had many, she admitted, seeing herself in the long mirror in her room. It was very nice, beautiful according to Maria, falling from just below her breasts to mid-calf length, the thin straps showing off her creamy shoulders and the well brushed shining silver of her hair. She wore no jewellery except the heavy silver bracelet that had been her mother's and the long silver earrings that had been a present from her father just before he had died.

She missed him tonight. She felt very much alone in an alien place and she could not really understand her misery, except that she felt as if she had cried, felt drained of emotion, her eyes bright as if in the aftermath of a storm of weeping.

She found herself placed between the Condesa and Miguel Hernandes, and felt a little more secure, like a book between two book-ends. The thought brought a smile to her face until she saw the Conde watching her and looked away rapidly from the coolly speculating eyes.

'You have met everyone except Señorita Martinez, I think, Sister Marsh?' he said before she could escape entirely. There was a cruel line to his mouth tonight and Laura felt her heart sink. To suffer the embarrassment of his quick, cruel tongue in front of strangers would be unbearable, and she had to remind herself forcefully that he too was a stranger, a stranger who would have no qualms about upsetting her.

'So, your nurse, Condesa Helen?' Carlota Martinez did not so much as look in Laura's direction. 'I do hope she's up to the task. You are rather naughty, you know, always doing things to make yourself ill.'

The patronising tones! She behaved as if she was the next Condesa de las Montanas already, and the Condesa put a trembling hand on Laura's arm. Whether she was trembling with anger or if she had been upset like this so often that the effects were instantaneous, Laura did not know, but her own misery left her as she looked with cool blue eyes at Rodrigo, waiting for him to intervene. He said nothing.

Carlota, however, was quite prepared to make up for his silence.

'She looks as pale as you do, Condesa. You should have had someone with a little more vim and vigour, shouldn't you?'

'I normally look pale and insipid,' Laura cut in, no longer caring whether the remarks were addressed to her or not. 'The Condesa does not need to be actually carried about. She needs perhaps a more tranquil atmosphere and less interference. Of course, if she wishes to see me glowing like a tulip, I can always paint my face like a clown!'

To say that the remarks dropped into a pool of astonished silence would have been an understatement. Carlota Martinez was quite a beauty, her dark hair thick and heavy, her clothes the most expensive that money could buy, but her lips were crimsoned to a degree that astonished Laura, and she wondered furiously if the Conde had had to wash his face after kissing her in such ardent welcome. Her make-up, too, was clever, and expensive, no doubt, but with the heavy hand of many people she had laid it on thick—with a trowel perhaps, Laura thought.

She met the thunderous gaze of the Conde with calm indifference and then, because he had made no move to protect his mother, because he had embarrassed her and kissed her into near imbecility, she had a go at him too.

'Is this the fork, Señor Conde?' she asked with sweet and cloying innocence, and began to eat her dinner.

Señorita Martinez was subdued thereafter and kept her remarks solely for the ears of the Conde. From time to time Laura raised her head to find him constantly watching her, his eyes narrowed and angry, threat in every line of his body.

She played bridge afterwards with the Condesa, Eduardo and Miguel Hernandes until the doctor said he would have to go. His reluctance was apparent, and Laura found him kissing her hand with the same grace that he bestowed on the Condesa.

'There goes the chance of charming him into any permission for an operation,' he said quietly, just as the Conde made an appearance with Carlota Martinez. Laura's eyes met the quizzical gaze of the doctor and she smiled ruefully.

'I'm afraid my tongue runs away with me sometimes,'

she confessed but he only smiled wider.

'You have only said what I would have liked to say for some time,' he assured her, 'though the remark about the fork was a little beyond me. However, beware, you will pay for it.'

She didn't doubt it. At the sight of her with Miguel, his hand still holding hers as he lowered it from his lips, she saw the Conde's face tighten and darken to anger.

She was to receive the brunt of it later as she went quietly to her room. The Condesa had begged her to see her to her suite and then had laughed until tears came to her eyes.

'I have been holding that laughter in all evening, Laura,' she admitted. 'You were what Rodrigo would have called *magnifico*! But he was as stunned as all of us. I heard him call you a silver dragon the other day. Now I know why. I have never been so happy and confident with that girl at dinner as I was tonight.'

The words were still in Laura's mind as she climbed the stairs, and she made her mind up then and there to battle it out. He was right, she *had* been about to desert her patient.

'Señorita Marsh!' The voice of doom! She halted and looked back down into the shadowy hall. 'A word with you, if you please.'

She did please, and marched back down the stairs as if she still wore her uniform. Better to get it over with after all, he was only a man.

The man, however, was not about to conduct his chastising of her in the great hall. He motioned her to a room which turned out to be his study. Huge and comfortable like all the other rooms, it was dominated by a wide mahogany desk and by the glowering presence of the master of the *castillo*.

He closed the door and strode over to the desk, turning and leaning against it with deceptive ease. He was furious, and there was no mistaking that. It would have been unnerving, but Laura's nerves were very good at the moment.

'You will explain why you found it necessary to be rude to Señorita Martinez,' he ground out at once. 'It is not your place to insult my guests!'

'It is my place to care for the Condesa. That is the only reason why I am here, and as you did not see fit to protect the Condesa from Señorita Martinez, then the task fell to me.'

'And the remark about the fork?' the Conde enquired threateningly.

'Sheer spite, *señor*,' Laura informed him tartly, beginning to enjoy herself.

'I am surprised that you bothered when you have stated that you will be leaving in the morning,' he said savagely. 'I would have thought you would have saved your strength for better things, Miguel Hernandes, for example.'

'Doctor Hernandes and I were having a professional chat,' she assured him coolly.

'Holding hands?' he rasped out.

'We were not! He was bidding me good night. As to leaving in the morning, I've decided to stay.'

'I see.' He was suddenly still and she knew he was thinking rapidly, wondering no doubt why his tricks were not working. It was alarming and a little hurtful to be disliked so much, it was something that had never happened to her before. She was accustomed to being well liked, to getting on easily with people, but he had disliked her on sight. Nobody that she could recall had ever done that before. She wondered what he would do now.

'And if I dismiss you after your insolent behaviour?'

'I shall sue you for breach of contract, Señor Conde, and I'm almost certain that the Condesa would support my claim. Probably Doctor Hernandes would too. He knows no doubt that your mother needs protection.

'Oh, I'm sure Doctor Hernandes would support you in almost anything, *señorita*. He is clearly ready to kneel at your feet.' The Conde suddenly moved from the desk to stand looking down at her straight, angry figure.

'So you think the Condesa needs protection, eh?' He raised a quizzical eyebrow. 'Let me tell you, *señorita*, that my mother is what can only be described as wily. She runs as many rings around us now that she is ill as she ever did when she was well. She is mistress of the *castillo* as she has always been, and I do not know what tale she has been telling you about Carlota, or what her cunning little reasons are, but had you not intervened on her behalf so bravely and hotly, you would have seen Señorita Martinez tied up in knots.'

'It will be different when you're married to the Señorita,' Laura exclaimed, thinking he probably discounted Carlota Martinez, but the Condesa certainly did not. 'You should think what the atmosphere will be like for your mother when there's a new Condesa.'

'When I marry Carlota?' he asked in surprise. 'Another idea that my mother has put into your head, or did you think that one out all by yourself?'

When Laura didn't answer, he stood silently for a minute, staring down thoughtfully into her pale face, seeming to be weighing his next words carefully before he spoke.

'My mother knows that sooner or later I must marry. It is my duty, although I have little desire for it. Still, I do not have the right to let my father's line die. An heir must be produced. If I had a brother, I would be greatly tempted to hand over the whole of my responsibilities to him, but as I have not, the duty rests with me.'

He turned away and went back to the desk, reaching for a cigarette and lighting it, watching the glowing end with thoughtful eyes, never looking at her.

'So she thinks that I have chosen Carlota? And she
does not like her. I do not wish my mother to be upset,
and who I marry is of little concern to me.' He suddenly
looked up, his dark eyes locking with hers. 'She likes you.
How would you like to take the job on?'

'What?' Laura's eyes were indeed like saucers.

'I believe you heard me and understood, Señorita
Marsh,' he observed quietly. 'I need to marry and
produce an heir. My mother is ill and the thought of
Carlota Martinez as the new Condesa is likely to make
her more ill than ever. She likes you. Marry me!'

'You—you're mad!' Laura stared at him in astonishment. Whatever she had imagined from this interview it
had certainly not been this. If this was another attempt to
get rid of her then she really couldn't see the plan at the
back of it. This time he had her completely astounded.
'You—you don't know me. You don't ask someone to
marry you just like that!' She knew that in some way that
she couldn't fathom he was being cruel again and that she
was saying all the wrong things, that she should have
simply laughed, but somehow she couldn't.

'Why do you not?' he enquired softly. 'I will soon get to
know you when we are married and you will get to know
me. You have known this David for some considerable
time and yet you hesitate to marry him. How long do you
intend to wait?'

'It's different,' she insisted, feeling as if she was caught
up in some sort of crazy dream. 'I—I wasn't sure if I
loved him enough to marry him.'

'And now you are?' he enquired coldly.

'No! Stop putting words into my mouth. The whole
idea is ridiculous, and I think it would be better if we
both agreed to forget that you ever suggested it—unless
of course you're once again amusing yourself at my
expense?'

'I am not,' he stated flatly, 'and I do not recall that I have ever amused myself at your expense, Señorita Marsh. You are not at all amusing, you are a source of constant irritation. Now, let us get on. I have asked you to marry me, properly, calmly and in all seriousness. I need an answer!'

He barked out the statement as if she was under police interrogation and she snapped back instantly. He had no idea how to behave rationally, he was consumed with his own importance, a woman was nothing, and she herself less than that, if it were possible.

'Then if you're serious, Señor Conde, the answer is no, definitely not. The whole idea is preposterous! Why me?'

'Why not you, *señorita*? I need an heir and there is only one way to get one. I must marry and have a woman legally in my life,' the Conde said with cold brutality. 'If you marry me it will still my mother's fears and settle my future all in one throw. You seem to be quite fond of my mother already, and having you constantly around the *castillo* would be good for her health. You could not of course continue as her nurse. You would be the Condesa de las Montanas with many other duties, not the least of which would be to produce an heir to the Castillo del Fuego and the estates.' His mouth twisted into a sardonic smile suddenly, his eyes holding hers. 'There would, however, be a little time that could be spared from that particular duty, and my mother would welcome your company and your friendship.'

Laura's face flushed hotly and she tore her astonished and embarrassed gaze from his.

'Now that I've listened to your proposal,' she stressed sarcastically, 'and now that you've heard my answer, I suggest, Señor Conde, that we get on with the purpose of my visit to your study, which was, I believe, the matter of my rudeness to Señorita Martinez.'

'You may be as rude as you wish to Señorita Martinez,'

he said with calm indifference. 'She does not concern me. She is in no way suitable to be the next Condesa de las Montañas.'

'And neither am I!' Laura cried wildly, looking up again in almost hysterical frustration, realising with sinking heart that now she would certainly have to leave Spain.

'You are most suitable, *señorita*,' he informed her coolly. 'In spite of the difference in our cultures, in spite of the difference in our ages, you are very suitable. Marriage is a nuisance, but I think that in your particular case it is a nuisance worth facing. I want you very badly.'

He said it with no emotion whatever, but the words themselves had the desired effect, and Laura's legs turned to water as she sank into the nearest chair.

'I—I . . .' She felt as if she was gasping for air, and the Conde watched her with a cold intensity that made it seem utterly impossible that he should have just made such a statement.

'You can't possibly . . . I don't understand . . .'

'You understand all too well, *señorita*' he remarked softly. 'I think you have understood for some little time, but you have been unwilling to take the idea out and look at it closely. In case you are indeed too young to realise what I mean, I will put it another way. I desire you. I have desired you from the moment that I saw you, and the feeling has grown to an urgency that, I confess, surprises me.' He walked slowly across to her, standing over her as she sat wide-eyed and trembling, frightening her to death.

'Do not be alarmed, *señorita*. Look at the whole thing logically. You are twenty-four. You have fled from your own country to seek a way of life different from the one you have been leading. Your application for the post stated that you have no relatives and you have since told me the same thing. What is to keep you in England

except a man you hesitate to marry? Here, you will be a
Condesa, mistress of the Castle of Fire. Your children
will be heirs to centuries of wealth and culture and, for
my part, my mother will relax and be happy, my heir will
be assured and I can forget about the whole vexing
problem.'

After one second of open-mouthed astonishment,
Laura sprang to her feet to confront him, her own face
white with fury.

'You can forget the problem? Is this your cold-blooded
idea of a successful marriage, Señor Conde? I expressed
the opinion once that there was more to marriage than
comfort. There's certainly more to marriage than the
expediency of solving a vexing problem!'

'There is love?' he enquired sardonically. 'That elusive
and overstated emotion so prized by women? I have told
you that I desire you. I have desired you since I first saw
you and lifted you into my arms.' The dark eyes bored
into hers. 'The desire grows more urgent with every
passing hour. It is a feeling stronger than love, *señorita*. I
have offered you marriage, the title of Condesa de las
Montanas and the right to rule my *castillo*. Surely that
meets with your approval? Surely it is honourable?' He
suddenly reached forward, pulling her against him. 'You
are afraid of marriage to me and the responsibility it
would bring? You would prefer that I simply take you?
You wish only to be my mistress?'

Laura stared into cold alien eyes, her body stiff and
terrified, telling herself that this simply could not be
happening. This was an old and cultured land; the Conde
was an educated man in spite of his leaning towards the
autocratic. But the eyes were eyes from the past, the arms
the arms of a conqueror.

'You wouldn't dare!' Even as she said it she
remembered Miguel Hernandes's assertion very clearly.

'If he wishes to do something, you may be assured, he will!'

'It is what I want,' the Conde reminded her in a soft, threatening voice. 'You respond to me so beautifully. You do not imagine, *señorita*, that I have failed to notice the fact? I think that there would be very little fight in you after the first few seconds. Would it not be best to be my wife? I will gladly keep you as my mistress, but then the rather annoying problem of my marriage would remain.'

'You—you're threatening me!' she gasped, unable to pull away. He had some strange power to subdue her and even now, in her fright, every part of her skin was tingling in anticipation of the moment when his lips would seek hers.

'Promising,' he corrected in a low voice. 'You want me. From the first moment I touched you, every part of you sprang to astonished life. You have put up very little resistance. We are ideally suited in that respect. You are willing.'

'It's not true!' She pushed frantically at the hardness of his chest, and his eyes darkened in anger as he let her go.

'It is true!' he rasped harshly, 'but I will give you time to become accustomed to the idea. We will talk about it later. You have had a long and trying day. Off to your bed, *señorita*, and think, as you go to your room, as you cross the great hall and climb the grand staircase, that all could be yours very soon. All you need to say is yes.'

'I am not greedy for possessions, Señor Conde,' Laura averred with more courage now that he had released her.

'I know you are not,' he agreed, 'or I would not perhaps be so ready to bestow them on you. You are beautiful and courageous. Will your courage stretch far enough to allow you to follow your desires, *señorita*, and belong to me?'

She stood for a second, meeting the dark determination of his eyes, her feelings swinging between relief and anxiety. He meant every word he had uttered. It was plain to see in his eyes, in the stance of his body, tense with suppressed excitement.

He was himself, a man out of time, ruthless and following his needs with a total disregard for the conventions of the century he lived in. At that moment, Laura felt grateful that she had been given any choice at all.

The brief tap on the door had her actually jumping with shock and she felt as if she had been pulled from a faraway alien world as the door opened and the Condesa came into the quiet study.

'I'm sorry, Rodrigo,' she said a trifle breathlessly, 'but I was sure Laura was here, and I really do need her.'

'What is it?' they asked the question almost simultaneously, the same anxiety etched in both their voices.

'I suppose—nothing,' the Condesa said apologetically, 'but I feel a little strange and I—well, I need Laura.'

'Let's go back to your bedroom.' Laura reached her side first, her own agitation dismissed as her natural calm and training took over.

'I will come.' The Conde moved determinedly to the door, but his mother looked at him a trifle anxiously.

'Please don't be hurt, darling, but I need Laura. She's so kind and tranquil and she knows what to do if . . . I honestly don't need any fuss or sympathy.'

Laura looked sharply at him, prepared to stop his steady advance by force if necessary, but he merely nodded his agreement, his eyes worriedly on the Condesa's pale face as he opened the heavy door for them.

'I will wait,' he said softly. 'Do not worry, *Madrecita*. I am neither hurt nor angry. I understand.'

The evening had been too much for her, Laura knew that. The presence of Carlota Martinez had either scared or angered her. The game of bridge had excited her and the long minutes of laughter, however enjoyable, had been a mistake. She needed a very different way of life if she was to survive.

The Conde was waiting outside, pacing about the hall as Laura came later from the Condesa's suite, and he turned to her at once.

'She is all right?'

'Yes and no,' said Laura, closing the door of the suite to keep their conversation as private as possible. She held up her hand as his face darkened to ready anger and to her surprise he was instantly silent.

'I'm not being facetious, Señor Conde,' she explained quietly. 'For now, yes, she is all right. I'm going to get changed and sit with her for a while. But, in the long term, she is definitely not all right, as you well know. Tonight's little heart tremors were brought on by very small things. She needs an operation, which I understand has been clearly explained to you several times, and she needs it now before it's too late.'

'It will also have been explained to you, Sister Marsh,' the Conde said with deadly quiet, 'that I will not risk her life in such an operation.'

'You risk her life daily, *señor*,' Laura interrupted firmly. 'Every hour of her life is passed in danger. She walks a tightrope between life and death with no safety net. Your permission for the operation would remove that danger.'

'And present her with a greater danger!' he ground out. 'You are here to bring her more security. You, *señorita*, are the safety net. You have calmed her. She asked for you rather than me—already she relies on you. I trust that you intend to stay here?'

'I do,' she said quietly. There was no way that she could abandon the Condesa. After tonight, she knew that her presence was a necessity. She wondered how the Condesa had survived so long, and she must somehow get the Conde to agree to the operation.

'Then let your stay be permanent,' he suggested softly, his shoulders relaxing. 'Agree to my proposal of marriage. It will make her happy and I cannot say that it will leave me indifferent.'

'I come from a very ordinary background,' said Laura, taking a deep breath and facing him squarely. 'My upbringing was sensible and rational and my training continued that theme. I do not indulge in fantasising and I would be obliged, señor, if you would let the matter drop.'

'My mother needs you here permanently, señorita,' he asserted, all the more sinister as he kept his voice lowered. 'And I need you as mother to my children. Doctor Hernandes has stated that you are strong and healthy and I am prepared to believe him, for in spite of your delicate appearance you have a fire to match the flames on the walls of the castillo. You are ideally suited to produce the Montanas heir and I want your fire in my arms as soon as possible. I can think of nothing that is unsuitable in a marriage between us.'

'You are not horse trading, Señor Conde!' Laura flared, shaking with rage at his cold-blooded, calculating reasons and pink with embarrassment at his suggestions. 'Your mother needs me only temporarily, as do any of my patients. I am not some kind of universal talisman! The Condesa needs an operation. Try to let that idea penetrate your arrogant mind! And you, Señor Conde, need urgent medical attention yourself; you're insane! People with delusions of total omnipotence are usually locked up and watched closely. Good night!'

She stormed away up the grand staircase, every movement of her body signalling rage, brushing past Carlota Martinez who stood halfway down the stairs watching with dark, angry eyes.

Only the unexpected sound of the Conde's delighted

laughter halted her progress as she turned for one furious glance to see him standing at the foot of the stairs, his face filled with admiration and alive with laughter.

He raised his hand to his lips in a final salute.

'*Magnifico!* Your fire will one day burn down the *castillo, señorita.* My resolve deepens by the second. We will talk tomorrow. *Buenas noches!*'

Laura turned and fled to her room as the Conde held out his hand to Carlota Martinez and led her out to the delightful cool of the evening air.

Laura donned her uniform the next morning. She had sat up very late, watching the Condesa until she was certain in her own mind that all was well, and the rest of the short night had been spent tossing between wild, erotic dreams of the Conde and terrifying nightmares of being pursued by a dark figure on a black horse. She awoke exhausted and heavy-eyed but determined to pull herself back into reality, a reality that the Conde, his mother and the very castle itself were pushing further into the distance every day.

She had resorted to what the Conde had called her cardboard fortress, and the dark eyes that surveyed her across the breakfast table acknowledged the fact.

Apart from a brief, '*Buenos días, señorita,*' he did not speak, and Carlota Martinez did not even bid her good morning. After eating so little that her appearance at the table was a complete waste of time, Laura rose silently and went in search of the Condesa, the Conde's dark eyes watching her as she left the room.

This morning the Condesa seemed well and the day took on what Laura hoped would turn out to be a normal routine: a few moments of conversation, a walk in the gardens and then the quiet, calming effect of her presence as the Condesa wrote letters and chatted endlessly in the intervals.

This time, Laura remained in the starchy security of her uniform and was startled and alarmed when, after lunch, the Conde appeared in his mother's suite to beg a favour.

'If you can spare her, I would like to show Sister Marsh some of the estate,' he coaxed with a charm that he obviously reserved for the rare occasions when orders would not do.

'What a good idea, darling!' The Condesa appeared to be delighted. 'I'm just going for my rest in any case, and Laura looks so pale and tired today. I feel so guilty about keeping her up last night. Do run along, both of you.'

Having been given no chance to intervene, Laura found herself in the hall looking at the self-satisfied face of her tormentor with suspicion and concern.

'You can ride?' he asked with all the appearance of normality.

'What?' She seemed to pass her time in this place moving from one astounding happening to the next.

'Do you ride?' he repeated patiently, his hand going up to test the stiffness of her cap, his eyebrows raised in surprise when he found it to be as unyielding as he had imagined. 'A horse,' he added in further explanation.

'Yes, but . . .'

'Good. We will ride to the foothills—the view of the estate from there is excellent. Change into something suitable and I will bring round Diablo and an animal less alarming for yourself.'

Laura stood still and opened her mouth, but he forestalled her.

'One, you have nothing to wear. Two, you are afraid of me, as I am insane, and three, you have no desire whatever to come.' He ticked off her excuses on his fingers, his eyes sharp and watchful, his lips twisting in amusement as she nodded stiffly.

'Perfectly correct,' she retorted, but he took her arm,

disregarding her wishes as usual.

'You can wear the becoming jeans that you wore yesterday as you rushed out to dig holes. You are in no danger from me because this morning I have altered my plans. Lastly, you look pale and tired and it may well do you a great deal of good. Come, I am asking you very nicely and I am filled with remorse at my behaviour of yesterday. Consider indulging me as you indulged my mother yesterday in the matter of gardening.'

They looked into each other's eyes and the Conde appeared to be utterly nonchalant, though she trusted him not one bit. She felt an overwhelming desire to get out into the open air, though, a desire that drowned her fear of being with him in the silent, lonely forest. Perhaps she was as mad as he, but she wanted to go.

'Very well, but I warn you, I haven't ridden since I was seventeen. I may fall off after the first few yards.'

'I am prepared to take the chance if you are, *señorita*,' he murmured quietly, and she wasn't at all sure what he meant. If he had been as he was the night before she would never have agreed to go. Even now, there was a light in his eyes that warned her that once again she had been lured out of her normal sensible attitude. She turned and left before he could see how scared she was, and his low chuckle of laughter did nothing to quieten her fears.

In the event, though, she was as excited as a child, hurrying to get out of the confines of her uniform and into jeans and low-heeled shoes. With the addition of a blue checked shirt, her outfit would pass muster, and on impulse she tied her hair into two bunches as she had done on the few occasions that riding lessons could be afforded at home.

To have told the Conde categorically that she could ride had, perhaps, been stretching the truth, considering the way that she had seen him ride Diablo across the sunlit clearing and later down the steep slopes to the castle. The idea had taken hold of her though and also, she admitted to herself, the excitement of spending some time in the company of the Conde was uppermost in her mind, in spite of her fears.

He was waiting in the courtyard at the back, tall and handsome in an outfit similar to the one he had worn when he had burst into her life such a short time ago: slim trousers, a black silk shirt and the attractive but alarming flat black sombrero, now hanging down his back.

'*Muy bien.*' His eyes roamed over her in approval, his gaze sensuous, and he saw the quick flare of annoyance in her eyes and smiled slowly, bringing her horse forward, Diablo's reins over his arm. 'Come, let us see you perform.'

The horse looked quiet, a dark mare with none of Diablo's temperamental appearance, and Laura offered silent prayers to any saint who happened to be tuned in, and mounted. Quite well as it turned out, causing the count to nod in satisfaction.

'*Bueno*, you can mount. Now let us see if you can remain in the saddle.'

He swung easily on to Diablo's back, his movements smooth and co-ordinated, a poetry of motion that had Laura watching him with the same approval that he had shown to her. He was an exciting, overpowering man, a man who could bring a thrill of fear to her or melt her towards him as he held her.

'We are ready, and I am overwhelmed at your approval of me, *señorita*.' He was watching her, seeing her eyes on him, and she flushed hotly as she met the intense gaze and the raised eyebrows. 'Your hairstyle is becoming and appreciated,' he added in a softly mocking voice. 'Knowing that you look like a silver-haired little girl no doubt makes you feel safe in my company, but do not be alarmed, I assure you that I mean you no harm.'

'Why did you ask me to come?' she asked uneasily as they turned to the great arch of the courtyard.

'You looked rather pale at breakfast and I knew you had spent a very uneasy time watching my mother last night. I thought that perhaps the fresh air of the mountains would revive you.' He slanted her a dark-eyed glance from beneath the brim of his sombrero, now tipped in arrogant style on his head. 'Also,' he added softly, 'in order to woo you.'

'What! Laura's startled exclamation had both her own horse and Diablo tossing restlessly, and instantly he nudged the great black horse close, his hand on the neck of the mare, soothing and quieting.

'That is the correct expression, is it not?' his voice mocked. 'You were affronted by my flat offer of marriage. You refused me, and emphasised that refusal by withdrawing into your own starchy castle. Very well, I will court you. I will behave as a suitor behaved in the days of my grandfather. We will leave your other possible role well in the background for the time being. Your hair is tied like a child's, your eyes are wide and blue. I imagine that this disguise will be effective enough to secure your safety—for today.'

She wished with all her heart that she had not agreed to come. A great burst of fear mixed with excitement raced through her and his eyes met hers as if he was reading her mind, his gaze steady and strange beneath the brim of the black hat, his figure straight and tall on the gleaming black horse, one hand resting low against the saddle, one resting on the strong curve of his thigh, silent, dark and dynamic. He was accustomed to winning and he saw no reason why he should pretend otherwise. Laura was a quarry to be chased down in the hunt and she knew that the hunt was all the more exciting to him because she was an intelligent prey.

'I will lead. Follow!' he said coolly, urging Diablo

through the great archway, and she felt he meant more than the ride that he had planned. He raised his hand in an uninterested salute of farewell to Carlota, who had appeared at the door, her face filled with anger, and Laura told herself that it was the Spanish girl's appearance that stopped her from dismounting then and there and hurrying back to what little security the Castle of Fire offered. As it was, she bit her lip anxiously and followed as the Conde had ordered, feeling in some panic-stricken way that she was allowing herself to be dragged from her own times into the cruel and barbaric past.

CHAPTER FIVE

Now they climbed upwards through the soft, grassy slopes and undergrowth that had so alarmed Laura on their descent when she had first come to the castle. The calm horse that she bestrode climbed surely and easily, seeking the best line, accustomed to the terrain. Seeing the Conde sitting easily with loose reins, allowing Diablo to pick his way steadily upwards, Laura did the same.

From time to time he turned to check on her, turning away after one swift glance until they were high in the forest. Then he waited, pointing out the superb view of the castle and grounds as she joined him.

It was hard to be uneasy in such beauty, and Laura realised as she gazed at the sunwashed glory of the castle that England had receded to the very back of her mind. In spite of the frequent anger that the dark, silent man beside her could arouse with very few words, there was a peace here and a tranquillity that had begun to seduce her soul.

The powerful and alarming Spaniard had become part of her life, and it suddenly dawned on her with a deep certainty that when she left this place, he would linger in her mind for ever. She could see herself back in England, in some hospital, her daily life one strict routine, her emotions under calm control, but the memory of Rodrigo, Conde de las Montanas never far from the front of her mind.

Already he haunted her dreams, already his dark presence filled her days. She was no longer in control of her life, for just as she thought she had achieved some normality, just as she had imagined that she had regained her normal calm, he was there, raging at her, coaxing her, threatening her or kissing her. He had pushed all thoughts of David out of her mind altogether. He had stormed into her life and had now announced his intention to stay there for ever.

For ever! It frightened and excited her, and she struggled to find some thread from the past to cling to, but found nothing that could force him from her mind. Was it to find this that she had escaped from England? Without even turning her head she could visualise every one of his features, could see the deep, exciting darkness of his eyes, the black gloss of his hair, the powerful perfection of his body.

She turned quickly to look at him, hoping to find herself mistaken, but her heart leapt yet again at the sight of him and with a feeling of destiny she realised with absolute certainty that the 'for ever' he offered was the 'for ever' she would have wanted if he had loved her.

He was watching her silently and intently, and she turned quickly away, her cool and beautiful profile the only sight of her face left to him.

'You have frightened yourself with some thought,' he asserted softly. 'Certainly I know that it is not I who have frightened you this time.

'Perhaps your very presence frightens me, *señor*,' she said flatly, turning the horse away from the bewitching sight of the castle, a sadness flooding over her that was at variance with her normal character.

'Perhaps,' he agreed quietly. 'I have said before that we are very different, you and I, *sol y sombra*, but I cannot be held responsible for my appearance. As Miguel Hernandes has said, we are all at the mercy of our genes, and I know you will believe him, *señorita*. Today I know that my behaviour is not in any way alarming.'

'How do you know?' Laura asked contrarily, angry for

the moment that he could make her feel so much by doing
so little.

'How could my behaviour be anything but excellent?'
he enquired with cool mockery. 'I am wooing you,
señorita.'

He set Diablo at a canter, urging him up into the
higher reaches of the sun-drenched forest, and Laura
followed more slowly. He was perfection to see, he was
arrogant, unkind, impossible, but in her heart she new he
would never be out of her bloodstream. He was part of
the magic of the land, a being who had stepped out of the
deepest reaches of her dreams, and she followed him
with a heavy heart, climbing through the forest,
following the blaze of the sun, the purple slopes of the
sierras, white-crested and invincible in the distance,
riding behind him as if she followed her destiny. He
would never know how she felt; she would certainly
never agree to his cold-blooded suggestion of marriage.
Sanity warned her not to put herself in his power in any
way. He was capable of tenderness, but he could not
examine her dreams, no matter how dark his probing
eyes. It was enough that she was a victim of her own
sudden and overwhelming love for him; he would never
discover that.

It was an afternoon that Laura knew would remain in
her heart forever. The Conde was a quiet courteous
companion, pointing out the vast sweep of the estate,
calling their horses to stillness so that she could watch the
deer that flitted like shadows beneath the trees, leading
her to the lower slopes of the sierras where the eagle
soared in magnificent and undisputed reign.

There were waterfalls that fell in silver cascades beside
the narrow paths, banks of wild flowers that grew to the
edges of the mountain streams and everywhere the heat
of the sun and the tranquillity of the mountains.

They turned for home in good time, re-entering the

forest, walking their mounts. There had not been endless
talk between them, but Laura felt almost a part of the
tall, dark man who walked with silent step beside her.

'*Momento*' He stopped her suddenly, his eyes on her
mount, a peaceful mare with the beautiful name of
Morena. 'She has trouble, I think.'

She had. As the mare moved restlessly, Laura saw that
she limped badly and he lifted her left foreleg, grunting
with annoyance.

'A stone, too deep I'm afraid for me to remove now.
She will have an uncomfortable walk to the *castillo*; we
are still far off.'

'Oh, poor thing! I'll walk with her. She can't carry me
and walk on a bad foot.'

'She cannot,' the Conde agreed. 'But if you walk back,
señorita, Morena is not the only one who will need
attention to her feet. I do not think that you realise just
how far we have come. Besides, if you walk then so must
I, and I have no fancy for it. Up you go!'

Before she could protest, he had taken her by the waist
and swung her up lightly on to Diablo, whose instant
reaction earned him this time a quick growl from his
master.

He looped the reins lightly over the mare's neck,
leaving her to follow at her own pace and then once again
he was astride the black horse, pulling Laura to him, a
repetition of the first time they had met.

'You are here again, *señorita*,' he observed with
amusement. 'The devil beneath you and the the devil
behind you—that is how you think of us, is it not?'

'I try not to think of you at all, Señor Conde,' she
answered in what she hoped was a firm voice.

'And you fail miserably, *señorita*,' he pronounced, the
humour dying from his voice.' However, you may stop
trembling, you are quite safe.'

In spite of her determination to remain upright and

aloof, in spite of the alarm racing through her, Laura
found that after a few yards she was once again seduced
into moving against him to match the movement of
Diablo, and she should really have felt no surprise when
his arm tightened round her and his head bent to allow
his lips to trail across her cheek.

'Don't!' She tried to jerk upright, but the arm around
her tightened like a steel band as his lips wandered
seductively to the curve of her neck.

'Why not?' he enquired coolly. 'Do not forget that I am
supposed to be wooing you. What does a man do in
England when he is courting a girl—sit in the parlour and
exchange brief, written memos?'

'You shouldn't talk like this, about wooing me, it's
idiotic!' Laura moved her head and he allowed her to
escape him, raising his head with a quiet laugh.

'If you wish me to be silent then I will be,' he promised
with quiet mockery. 'I prefer to be a man of action, it is
my nature, my genes again. Be warned, however,
señorita, you will remember the actions long after you
have forgotten the words.'

Silenced by such subtle threats, Laura kept still, like a
mouse who aims to avoid the cat by pretending not to be
there at all, and her reward was a burst of laughter from
her tormentor as he raised his hands to her hair, freeing
the bands that held it and tucking them into the front of
her shirt with seductive slowness.

'Let me see your silver banner flowing free in the
sunlight!' he ordered firmly. 'When you marry me in the
white, virginal simplicity of the Montanas bride, the
whole congregation of the cathedral will gasp at your
fairness and beauty.'

'I shall not be here to see it, Señor Conde,' she said, her
whole body trembling and aware.

'Do not be so ready to dismiss the idea,' he warned in
quiet, threatening tones. 'Were it not for the annoying

problem of an heir to the Montanas estates, I would not be sitting so readily on Diablo. We are far from the *castillo*, alone in the depths of the forest. A wedding in the cathedral takes a tiresome amount of arranging for one of my family, an eternal wait of several weeks. You could more easily be my mistress and I would not have to wait beyond the next few minutes. I feel your slender body tremble against me, and though I realise it is almost wholly from fear, there is still an excitement in you that tells me that you are far from unwilling. You may imagine that I am the devil himself, but at this moment I am only aware that I am a man, frustratingly close to my desires. It would perhaps be best if we remained silent and enjoyed the scenery; certainly it would be better for you, *señorita*.'

He whistled softly to Morena, who limped behind them as he set Diablo to an easy walk that would not tax the dark mare too much, and Laura took the advice, trying to still her trembling. By the time they rode under the courtyard arch, her whole body was stiff with anxiety and the constant fight to remain upright and as far away from him as possible.

To imagine that Carlota had been at the door since their departure was ridiculous, but the unlikely thought did occur to Laura as they entered the courtyard and she saw the Spanish girl watching them. At any other time, Laura would have laughed at the bewildering mixture of expressions that moved swiftly across the girl's face— jealousy, anger and satisfaction, the reason for the last becoming apparent as soon as she spoke.

'Can't she ride after all, Rodrigo?' The way that the girl constantly ignored her made Laura wonder if she had attained invisibilty to some people.

'She rides,' he answered shortly. 'Morena has picked up a stone. But it is not the first time that Diablo has carried both of us, nor I expect will it be the last. His uncertain temper is going to have to improve or I may well need another horse.'

Laura had no way of telling if his remarks were a subtle way of telling Carlota to mind her own business or if he was intent upon restating his intentions with regard to herself. At any rate, her cheeks flushed hotly and, for the first time ever, Carlota looked at her directly, her eyes filled with hatred.

There was nothing of the suitor in the way that the Conde looked at her as he lifted her to the ground, however.

'You should soak in a hot bath,' he advised cynically. 'For the last few miles you have been sitting as stiffly as your small white cap. One would imagine that you, too, have been starched!'

'I know how I feel, thank you,' Laura said quietly, embarrassed that Carlota was coming closer, intent on hearing their quiet and cold conversation.

'So do I,' he stressed harshly. 'You are swinging between desire and fear. A few nights in my arms will sort out both those feelings. The sooner that we settle our future, the better it will be for both of us.'

'We have no future, Señor Conde!' she asserted, distressed to find that the thought brought only sadness.

'The future that we have is entirely up to you,' he rejoined coldly. 'But make up your mind, I will not wait for ever. At the moment you have freedom of choice; delay much longer and I will make up your mind for you, and you will then have no fears about the awesome duties that will befall you as Condesa de las Montanas—your duty will be only to please me.'

He was watching her coldy and she stared silently back, unable to point out to him that she was free to do as she liked, free to leave the castle and Spain. She was once again the quarry, cornered and waiting.

'I will see to the horses. Run along to your bath,' he

grated with a sudden frown of frustration, reducing her to the state where she would either have to trot off with childlike acceptance, or reply with equally childish tantrums.

'I'll come with you to the stables, Rodrigo,' Carlota said firmly, arriving at their side, and he turned to her with a charming smile that had been totally absent when he had spoken to Laura.

'By all means—I have seen little enough of you this visit. Come and talk to me while I see what can be done for Morena.'

They simply walked off and Laura turned as she reached the door to see his arm across Carlota's shoulders, their heads close together, the rapid flow of Spanish quite beyond her. The memory of the way he had kissed Carlota on her arrival was suddenly very close, and a burst of wild jealousy tore through Laura, only to be determinedly squashed. They were well suited, perfectly alike. Two of a kind, she thought angrily, and nothing to do with her. She stormed off to her room, angry, jealous and utterly frustrated.

With an infantile desire to disobey every order or suggestion that he made, she simply showered and dressed in white skirt and deep peach blouse. There was a growing fury inside her that had to be worked off somehow and rather than bottle it in until dinner time, when she would once again have to face Carlota, she went out into the garden to walk off her anger between the tall hedges and the fountains.

The walled garden was cool in the early evening, the trickle of the fountains a solace as she walked between the clipped hedges where the jasmine spilled in a cascade of blossom on to the paved path. Laura noticed nothing, however; she was too disturbed inside to appreciate the beauty. The only thought in her mind was the necessity to escape from the castle and the Conde before her heart won the battle and she stayed for ever.

There was also the problem of the Condesa. She was, after all, a patient in need of care and, in any case, Laura had rapidly become fond of her and the thought of deserting her and never knowing how her health progressed lay heavily on her conscience.

The sight of Miguel Hernandes in front of her brought her to a startled halt. Obviously he was looking for her and, though she wanted no company, her professional attitude took over at once.

'Is something wrong with the Condesa?' She should have been in to see her instead of thinking all the time about the Conde.

'No, no.' He waved a hand in a calming gesture. 'I saw you come out and wondered in fact if there was anything wrong with you. You appeared to be agitated. I wondered if you needed a doctor?' he added with a disarming grin.

'A psychiatrist, probably,' Laura admitted ruefully. 'I've been riding with the Conde.'

'Ah, perhaps a sedative?' They looked at each other with understanding and then both laughed.

'My dear Laura—I may call you that?' Miguel enquired politely, and smiled when she told him she would be glad if he did. 'Consider that any time in the company of the Conde may be time well spent for our patient's sake. A sacrifice for your profession, eh?'

She laughed, some of the tension leaving her at his wider outlook. Of course, he was not beginning to fall deeply in love with the Conde. He saw things very differently, but it was a relief to talk to him, to have an ally.

The sudden appearance of the Conde at the end of the path, once more changed into the beautiful casual clothes he wore around the castle, made Laura stiffen and wiped the smile off her face.

'Ah.' Miguel glanced round and then shrugged apologetically. 'This is the end of our chat, I believe.'

'You'll be there for dinner?' Laura asked a trifle anxiously, but he shook his head.

'No. I have a rather difficult case at the moment and must stay near the hospital. I was invited and declined. I rather think, also, that I was invited more to aid with the marshalling of the Condesa's forces against Señorita Martinez than for the pleasure of my company.'

He turned and nodded pleasantly at the Conde, who appeared to be about to explode into a temper.

'I will bid you goodbye then, Laura,' he smiled, not one bit overwhelmed by the towering presence of the Conde. '*Hasta la vista.*'

Laura was left to take the brunt of the Conde's sizeable temper and her eyes followed Doctor Hernandes wistfully. She would have liked to walk off, too.

'Your assignation with Miguel Hernandes is over so quickly?' he rasped as soon as she looked at him. 'I'm sorry I arrived so unexpectedly on the scene.'

'We were discussing our patient!' Laura said angrily, her own temper rising. She walked towards the fountain, but he followed.

'That excuse is becoming rather thin,' he snapped. 'Does he normally call his colleagues by their first names?'

'I imagine he does,' she replied sharply. 'He's a kind, considerate man.'

'Everything that I am not?' he enquired sarcastically. 'Is he so considerate that you can risk meeting him looking like that?' he ground out, his eyes running over her angrily.

'Like what?'

'It is clear that you are wearing very little beneath that skirt and blouse. If you appear like that it will be for my

eyes only, no matter what position you decide to occupy
in my life!'

She knew her blouse was thin, but the lacy bra beneath
was perfectly decent. She had worn the blouse in
England without drawing any speculative glances, but
she found her face heating with embarrassment.

'You have no right to make remarks about my person!'
She turned to glare at him, but embarrassment completely engulfed her and she found herself unable to meet his
eyes. 'In any case, I won't be . . .'

'Your person is making remarks to me,' the Conde
interrupted angrily, 'and I do not doubt that it was
making similar remarks to Doctor Hernandes!'

'I'll leave the castle tomorrow,' Laura avowed, her
head turned away from his dark gaze. 'There's no reason
I should have to put up with this sort of thing!'

'You know that such statements are very safe to make,'
he pointed out softly, 'because you know very well that I
will never let you go.'

His voice frightened her. There was possession in
every carefully chosen word, and she spun away, terrified
that he would see her face and realise how she felt about
him.

In her agitation, she didn't know where to run, where
to turn, forgetting for the moment their close proximity
to the fountain. Her foot caught the sculptured edge of
stone and but for his speed in grasping her arm she would
have fallen headlong into the water. As it was, she was
drenched down the front from head to waist, and she
turned gasping with shock at the impact of the cold water
that was fed from the mountain streams.

'Oh!' She wanted to blame him, but honesty told her it
was her own fault. Only now she was beginning to realise
why the Conde could so easily anger and distress her. She
wanted to be near him, wanted him to show her a
tenderness that was not in his character. This was why

her calm, her discipline, had deserted her.

Anything she would have rashly said, however, died on her tongue when she saw his eyes running over her with a look of obsession, his face tight, a muscle in his jaw moving spasmodically as if he was using enormous self-control.

He never spoke, and she looked down, following the gaze of the dark eyes that were riveted hotly on her, and saw just what the drenching had done. The silken top was clinging to her like a second skin, completely transparent from the soaking. The bra might well have not been there at all. Her breasts were hard and tight against the material, their darkened peaks more than any mere shadow in the clear evening light.

'Oh no!' She turned, but his hands shot out and grasped her shoulders, forcing her to face him again.

'Never before in my life have I wanted to take a woman to my bed on first sight of her,' he said softly. 'Do not be embarrassed—you have only revealed what my imagination told me the first time that I held you. I will not let you run from me. I want to look at you.'

Laura should have been struggling, fighting, but she could do nothing and there was sensuous passion in the hands that moved over her shoulders and found the heavy swell of her breasts, moulding them beneath his long powerful fingers, his face harsh with passion.

Her moan of pain and pleasure had him raising eyes that were dazed with desire to her flushed and appealing face. She wanted to beg him to allow her to escape, but the look on his face stilled her tongue.

'You are not angry that I touch you,' he breathed thickly. 'You are a litle afraid, but you are not angry, and I want to touch every part of you. I have been wanting you like this since I found you in my forest.'

He semed to be hovering over her, dark and powerful as an eagle soaring over the sierras, his eyes holding her as he continued to fondle her, his face alive with pleasure, his lips breathing over hers.

Suddenly he slid his arms tightly around her, pulling her to him and tilting her face up to his.

'You are unused to this,' he asserted with a satisfied certainty. 'No one has touched you before. You are innocent and afraid, warm and alive in my hands, throbbing with feelings that you do not understand fully.' His lips wandered over her heated skin as he whispered softly to her, his hands stroking her into mindless enchantment. 'I will teach you to understand, and soon there will be no fear in you.'

The lips that captured hers were fiercely insistent and her mouth opened beneath his with fatalistic acceptance. She had lost all identity, all reason given up to the lovemaking of a man she hardly knew, who alarmed every fibre of her being but who could draw her to him with one look. He recognised her ensnarement, and she heard deep sounds of satisfaction in his throat as he plundered her mouth, his hands moving over her with fiery pleasure.

Mindless of her wet clothes that soaked into the light cashmere sweater that he had donned against the cooler evening air, he pressed her to his hard urgent body, forcing her to accept the evidence of his desire as his lips trailed a heated, sensuous track from her neck to the deep swell of her breasts.

'*Dios!*' he groaned against her bruised lips. 'I want you now! How long must I wait until you lie in my arms, before I taste every part of you?'

'Please, *señor!*' Laura's hands trembled against his face and even to her own ears it sounded ridiculous to be addressing with such formality the man who had plundered her very being. It brought a breath of sanity to him, had him smiling down at her as he drew his head back to gaze at her winsome face.

'Will you still be calling me *señor* when you are lying in my bed?' he enquired softly.

'I won't be . . .' She shook her head wildly, but he grasped her chin, his other hand still forcing her against the hard length of his body.

'You will be!' he grated fiercely. 'We both know that. I am starving for you. We are miles away from anyone who does not owe allegiance to me. Refuse to marry me and I will take you!'

'The Condesa would not permit . . .'

'The Condessa will not know,' he assured her grimly. 'You are too much of a nurse to risk her health by begging her assistance.'

'You—you wouldn't!' Laura found the strength to struggle and, to her relief, he let her go.

'I want you,' was all he would offer in mitigation of his crimes. 'It is a feeling that overrides all others, even your so-called love. I do not normally wait for things that I want and I have another castle not too far from here. It is not so beautiful, but it is isolated and secure. Refuse me and I will take you there.' He looked at her with angry possession. 'Fight me any more and I will forget the matter of the Montanas heir. The need to continue the line of my ancestors fades into nothing when I look at you.' His hand came out to stroke down her face and his eyes stared threateningly into her. 'I am tempted to ignore my offer of marriage,' he whispered silkily, his face still and dark. 'I am tempted to take you from the *castillo* tonight and keep you to myself in the castle beyond the mountains.'

They stared at each other in silence, and Laura was unable to move. She knew that she should be running, escaping from the gardens and from the castle itself, but his eyes held her in bondage and her legs trembled too much to risk flight.

'Enough!' He pulled off the beautiful cashmere

sweater and slipped it over her head, freeing her hair from the neckband with suddenly gentle hands. 'I am reminded that when I first saw you I thought that you were almost a young girl and in no way a woman. You are a fraud, are you not, Laura? Your anger used to mask your desire and I frighten you more with every word I utter, with everything I do.' He paused in his purposeful determination to dress her in the warmth of his sweater, cupping her head with strong hands. 'Marry me. It will drive the devil from me and you will learn soon enough not to fear me. I will protect you always. You are not indifferent to my caresses. You burn with a fire of your own, and as for me, I feel that I have known you before, desired you before, as if time has run backwards to some distant place where I am at peace.'

His words struck a deep chord within her. There was somehow a plea for help, and she remembered her sad thoughts that he was a man out of time, as alien to his own people as he was to her. The thought made her eyes suddenly fill with tears and he looked down at her with strange dark eyes.

Do you weep for yourself or for me, I wonder?' he asked quietly. 'If it is for yourself, then I am sorry, but I need to possess you. If it is for me, then I do not want your pity. I want your silken softness beneath me for as far into the future as I can at this moment imagine.'

He bent his head and kissed her breasts through the wet transparency of her blouse before pulling her arms through the sleeves of the sweater, enclosing her in the warmth that had radiated from his body.

She was incapable of helping herself and stood like a rag doll in his hands, weak and trembling, her body alive and glowing in the aftermath of his passion. He looked down at her with a gentleness that she could not believe.

'Come,' he ordered softly. 'Let us get you indoors before you catch a chill.' His hands came firm and sure to lift her face. 'You will soon find that I can make you happy, Laura,' he promised. 'We amuse each other, even though we fight bitterly, and sexually we are like a raging fire. What else do we need? You could not go away and marry a man who has never raised you to the heights of passion that you have felt in my arms. Do you imagine that you could forget me, or that I would allow you to go? If you feel that you need to escape, remember that I will find you and bring you back. These little skirmishes are merely wasting time that could be spent more pleasurably.'

He walked back with her to the castle, his hand on her arm in a manner that left her in no doubt that he meant what he had said. He did not intend that she should leave the Castle of Fire.

He met Maria's astonished looks as they entered the great hall with a blank stare.

'The *señorita* has fallen into the fountain,' he said crisply as he saw Laura's distress. For himself she knew that he would have offered no explanation and she felt perhaps she should be grateful that he had bothered now. He did not enquire why Maria was hovering about the hall, but she answered the unspoken question in his eyes before he could become angry.

'There has been a telephone call for Sister Marsh,' she explained quickly. 'It was a Doctor Elliott, and he will ring again in half an hour.'

'*Bien!*' The Conde's expression belied the word. 'You will bring tea for the *señorita* and I in the study while she changes. She will take the call there.'

Her affairs in determined hands, Laura had to accept, and she went to change with the memory of his passion still flooding through her and his cold disapproval of her telephone call still in her mind. She had no alternative but to return to the study to face him, but she lingered until she thought that it would be time for the call, returning to the study to find him just answering the phone.

'Your call.' He handed the phone to her and walked out, ignoring the tea which had clearly been growing steadily more cold as she lingered in her room, and Laura lifted the receiver to answer nervously when the well-known voice came on the line.

'Laura? That was quick. Were you waiting, darling?'

The shock of the endearment made Laura realise just how much she had changed in such a brief time. It was almost as if a stranger had addressed her in loving tones, and her answers to his eager questions were brief and forced. Her feelings now were deeply rooted in the Castle of Fire, her heart given to a ruthless man, a near-stranger who pursued her relentlessly.

Even as David was speaking, her mind was with Rodrigo, fearful because she felt the great temptation to agree to marriage, her foolish heart asking her if it would not be better to marry him without his love rather than never see him again. There was the thrill of his desire for her, and here in the old castle it did not seem so unreal, so unacceptable, as it would have seemed in the harsh modern world she had left.

'Did you hear what I said, Laura?'

She came to herself to find that she had missed at least half of the conversation and that David seemed to realise it. She was still flushed and breathless from her earlier meeting with the Conde, still mentally in his arms in the quiet garden, and nothing else had any reality.

'I—no, I missed it. It's a bad line,' Laura finished lamely.

'I said I had a few days due and I'm coming out to see you.'

'No!' It was out before she could stop it and her fear was real. What the Conde would do when confronted with David she did not dare to think. Already he had the fixed idea that Miguel Hernandes was a possible rival. David's positon in her life was very real.

'For God's sake, Laura! When is this nonsense going to end? Look, I'm coming out and you can meet me anywhere you choose or I'll come to the castle to see you. It's time we were married, or at the very least officially engaged. You'll come to your senses when we're together.'

Laura hardly heard the rest of the conversation. Her own remarks seemed to be nothing more than pleas to have David remain in England. They were ignored.

She put the phone down with trembling hands, unsure as to what arrangements they had finally made. All her senses seemed to be leaving her. She wasn't even sure any more if she was a good nurse. All she could think of was the terrible scene that would result from a visit from David, and she leaned against the desk, her hands covering her face.

'He has upset you!'

She spun round to find the Conde in the doorway, his face thunderous.

'You listen in to other people's telephone conversations?' she asked shakily, miserable and embarrassed.

'Only when the conversation interests me,' he assured her coolly, coming over to her. 'And I can see that he has upset you.'

'He says he's coming out here to see me.' She might as well tell him now and get the fury out into the open. Better to face it now than live in dread of it. 'He wants to—to get engaged at once. He says it's time we were married and . . .'

Her voice trailed away at the laughter on his face. Whatever she had expected it had not been this.

'And your repeated answer was no.' He looked very satisfied with himself. 'There is much to be said for listening in to other people's telephone conversations, I

think.' His dark eyes were dancing at the look on her face
and he added softly, 'Now why should it upset you so
much that he wishes to come here? Most girls would be
delighted that two men were pursuing them, or, in your
case, three.'

'If you mean Doctor Hernandes . . .'

'Hush, Laura. Am I not allowed to tease you
sometimes? And do not be so upset. If he wishes to come
then let him. I cannot say that he will be welcome, but
you are entitled to have visitors. You are neither a
servant nor a prisoner.'

'He wants to meet me some place, otherwise he'll come
here,' Laura told him.

'If you prefer, I will drive you to some meeting place,
or you can meet him here. It really does not matter very
much, surely?'

'Why are you being so nice to me?' She looked at him
with more awe than suspicion, and he laughed softly, his
hand coming up to brush the still damp hair from her
face.

'Should I not be nice to you when I am wooing you?' he
mocked softly. 'If I felt that this man was a threat, then
my attitude would be very different, but I have just held
you in my arms. I know how you feel and your eyes are
telling me even now. It is only your stubborn little mind
that needs assistance. You have seen the portraits of my
ancestors that decorate the walls of the grand staircase?
In those days, you would have been carried up the stairs
and your mind made up for you. I do not feel so very
different from those lost times. I find the rules and
regulations of my own times irksome and stupid. I have
already ascertained your feelings, and the delay makes
me impatient.' His hand captured her face with
imperious determination. 'If I carried you to my room
now, if I decided to make up your mind for you, you
would be tranquil in the morning, your fears ended, your

desires fulfilled. I am but a breath from doing it when I look into your blue eyes, but I will wait for your decision.'

'I—I' haven't said anything about marrying you, except to tell you that I will not,' Laura reminded him anxiously, her face rosy at the picture he painted. 'I hardly know you, and I know that you dislike me, *señor*.'

'Rodrigo,' he corrected softly, his eyes roaming over her face, seeing the distress there. 'I dislike your temper, I dislike your ability to defy me and your stubborn determination to have your own way, but that is all. There can only be one master in the *castillo* and there can only be one master for you. I relish the thought of taming you; my only annoyance now is that I cannot begin to tame you tonight, this moment. And you will marry me, or I will be your lover, for as long as you please me. The choice open to you is simple. Make the choice soon. I have warned you of my impatience.'

He suddenly laughed and took her arm, urging her gently to a chair.

'Come, I have rung for fresh tea. I'm sure you are in need of it after your worrying telephone call. This time, you will sit here and serve it to me and we will talk calmly. This time you will get no chance to hide in your room while I wait impatiently for a sight of you.' He shot her a narrow-eyed glance of amusement as she flushed. 'I find it relatively easy to follow the track of a stubborn mind, Laura,' he said softly. 'I have a stubborn mind myself. Remember that when you are preparing to defy me. Ask yourself what you would do if you were utterly ruthless and, be assured, I would do it.'

CHAPTER SIX

RODRIGO'S good humour lasted for several days, days when Laura's feelings moved between near happiness and uneasiness. Since the incident at the fountain he had not attempted to touch her; the whole matter had been allowed to drop. He was charming and courteous to both herself and Carlota, but Laura now knew him well enough to realise that he was merely biding his time. His repeated insistence that she call him by his first name had had the desired effect, especially as he now addressed her as Laura and his firm correction when she addressed him as Señor Conde was, as often as not, conducted in public. Even the frequent visits of a very friendly Miguel Hernandes failed to bring a frown to his face, and a state of tranquillity filled the castle.

One morning, however, she found the Condesa distressed, clearly unwell, and, as her own relationship with the Conde now made it seem feasible, she determined to seek him out and put the matter of the operation to him again.

She was standing in the hall, undecided whether to face him in his study or wait until the matter could be mentioned at a more suitable time, when he pounced on her.

'Good! If you are wandering around the *castillo* with nothing to do, you can take coffee with me.'

Laura swung round quickly to find him towering over her, dark and vibrant. The fear that she had felt at the sight of him in the forest and the now familiar and constant leaping of her heart when she saw him combined to bring on a bewildering attack of vertigo, and she swayed unsteadily, her hands to her breast.

'What is it? You are ill?' Rodrigo's voice was sharp with anxiety and she felt his arm come round her.

'No, I'm all right. You startled me, that's all.'

'You mean that I frightened you.' he corrected coldly, his arm falling away. 'Do not spare my feelings, please. I am well aware that I frighten you, often terrify you. I suppose that I can expect nothing else when we are so different. I imagine that it is a state I will have to learn to live with. Normally, you have time to compose your face, a trick I suppose you learned long ago in your profession, but now I have appeared unexpectedly and you react purely instinctively, with fear. The fear must indeed be great with one so fiery as you, that my appearance can reduce you to trembling.'

He was stiff and angry, immediately back into his cold aristocratic shell, and Laura was unable to think of anything that would set matters right. No denial would satisfy him.

She longed to tell him that any fright she felt was now only because of her love for him and the growing certainty that she would never leave the castle, that she would be unable to resist his determination, even knowing as she did that it stemmed from nothing more than desire and expediency.

She told him nothing, however. He was once again the Conde, powerful, arrogant and cold, a man so far beyond her that his vows of desire now seemed unbelievable.

'You have the necessary nerve to enter my study for coffee?' he enquired sarcastically, and Laura bit her lip rather than retort with harsh words of her own. She had a mission, and now was as good a chance as any. He was not likely to return to the gentle ways of the last few days. She had convinced him by her actions that he was nothing more than a tyrant in her eyes.

'Certainly. I wish to talk to you anyhow.'

He nodded and led the way, remaining silent until coffee was brought and served, never even glancing at her until the maid had closed the door and left.

'Talk away, then, *señorita*,' he invited, his eyes coldly appraising her, his return to the formality of their previous relationship making her heart sink.

'The Condesa is unwell today.'

'I know it. I've seen her. She is often unwell. It is a sad reality that we live with. It is true that under your care she has improved, but she will never be well completely again. It is something that you must accept as you will see her like this for the rest of her life. As I say, it is a reality that we live with, a reality that you must learn to live with.'

'It's an unnecessary reality,' Laura said ardently. 'There are doctors in England who are performing the operation that she needs almost daily, as a matter of course. I'm sure there are doctors in Spain who could do the operation with equal success.'

'No!'

Laura stared at him in disbelief. Clearly he wasn't even prepared to give the matter any thought.

'You can't just say "no" like that! This is her life we're talking about.'

'A life that means more to me than you can possibly imagine,' Rodrigo cut in harshly. 'I am well aware that in your frequent discussions with Miguel Hernandes the Condesa's proposed operation has been given priority. However, I do not propose it! The responsibility of everything here rests on my shoulders, including the responsibility for my mother's continued existence. I must ask myself what my father would have done, and I do not need a crystal ball. He loved her, he would have done everything in his power to keep her. He would have taken no risk, no fifty-fifty chance.'

'Even if he condemned her to being an invalid for the

rest of her life, a happy bubbling mind trapped in a body that refuses to function properly? Is that love? In any case, you will lose her, it's only a matter of time.'

'What time she has will be spent here with those who love her!' he answered flatly, his eyes black and unemotional.

'Like a bird trapped in a cage? I'm not surprised that you think love is a foolish dream, Señor Conde,' Laura retorted, her eyes wide and accusing. 'You have no conception of it. To you it's merely hanging on to the things that you find convenient, including people!'

'You are referring to yourself too, I imagine,' he said with a quiet anger that was clearly growing by the minute. 'I have never professed to love you. I desire you, but at this moment, Sister Marsh, I could easily kill you. You are turning over stones that are best left lying, you are bringing to the top of my mind that which is a constant wound and you are rubbing salt into it with your ready tongue. You are as stiff and starchy as your tidy uniform.'

'I'm pleading for my patient!' His words hurt more than he could possibly tell. 'I can't stay here and quietly watch her deteriorate. I won't be here when she dies, knowing that it's such a cruel and needless waste of a wonderful and beautiful life!'

'So you are in fact threatening me?' he concluded softly. 'If I do not agree to this operation, you intend to leave Spain and escape back to your neat, efficient, sterilised world?'

'I have no intention of threatening you,' Laura snapped, her own temper rising. 'I've never said I would even consider marrying you. All the decisions in that direction have come from you. Well, you may have the right, or imagine that you have the right, of life and death here, but you have no rights as far as I'm concerned. If I can't do my job, then my time here is simply a waste of my training and inclinations. I would resign from any hospital where the patients were simply allowed to die!'

'You little . . .'

She never found out what Rodrigo had intended to call her or what his actions would have been, because as he sprang to his feet with blazing eyes, there was a sharp knock on the door and Maria stood rather anxiously in the doorway at the Conde's curt call of '*Adelante!*'

'There is a vistor, Señor Conde.'

'Then show the visitor in,' he snapped. 'You are supposed to be the maid of Sister Marsh and not available for other duties. Why are you answering the door?'

'The visitor is for Sister Marsh,' said Maria with a worried glance at Laura. 'It is an English gentleman.'

Rodrigo turned with one swift movement, his face like ice, and Laura caught some of Maria's fear to add to her own. He had said that she was entitled to visitors, but the sight of his face showed only too clearly that he did not wish her to see any English gentleman, and she suddenly knew with sinking heart who it would be. David had told her he intended to come, and there was a stubbornness about him that would have had him boarding the first plane that was available when his duties at the hospital were over.

As the Conde strode from the room, Laura felt her heart sink like a stone. David could not have picked a worse time to arrive; the Conde was in the most raging temper she had ever seen. After one panicky look in her direction, Maria fled from the vicinity, and Laura would have liked to flee with her.

But the sight of the tall form, the well-known shock of fair hair and the quizzically smiling face of David filled her with relief and brought back a little sanity to an unthinkable situation. Her pleasure at seeing him was very apparent, and when he strode forward and clasped her possessively in his arms, she did not resist.

'What are you up to?' He held her at arm's length and looked at her severely. 'I got the distinct impression that you heard about a quarter of my phone call. You were supposed to phone me back and arrange a meeting.'

'I—I forgot.' Laura looked at him with pleading eyes, and he grinned and shook his head.

'What became of the super-efficient Sister Marsh? And you forgot all about me? Thanks a million!'

'I'm really sorry, David. You've come all this way.'

'I know!' He suddenly laughed, easygoing again as usual. 'Lovely journey, though. Where can we talk?'

'You may talk here, Doctor Elliott.' Rodrigo was standing in the doorway, his eyes on the arm that David kept firmly around Laura's shoulders. 'I will leave you to your discussion in my study, unless you prefer to go elsewhere?' he added, his eyes unreadable as he looked at Laura.

'There's a sizeable town not too far away,' David intervened quickly before Laura could speak. 'I came up the coast road. I'll take you there for lunch, darling, if you're free?'

'She is perfectly free to do as she pleases,' the Conde said coldly, his eyes narrowed and blazing at the sound of the endearment said with the ease of familiarity. 'How will she return?'

'I'll bring her, of course.' David looked surprised. 'I'm booked into a hotel there. We can eat in the dining-room and then go up to my room to talk.'

Laura thought this intimate suggestion was about to bring forth an explosion of rage. David had no idea of the relationship that existed between herself and Rodrigo and she knew that today she would have to tell him. She knew, too, that today she would have to give Rodrigo her answer, and she had decided what it would be. There was no way that she could stay here now, seeing the Condesa get worse, loving Rodrigo and being constantly reminded that he loved her not at all. It was time to leave.

She went to change and was just coming from her room, fresh and cool in a blue cotton dress that matched her eyes, her legs long and slender beneath the billowing skirt, when she almost bumped into Rodrigo, who was waiting in the corridor. Clearly, his Spanish courtesy had not stretched to staying to talk politely to David.

'You will come back?'

Laura looked at him quickly. For one second she imagined there had been a plea in his voice, but the eyes that looked down at her were cold as the mountain streams that fed the fountains.

'Naturally,' she affirmed, her voice matching his eyes in icy indifference. 'My clothes and belongings are here and my contract is still not fulfilled.'

'You will tell him that you are to marry me!' he said harshly.

'I'll tell him nothing of the sort! I've never led you to believe I intend to marry you!'

'You have not said the words yet,' Rodrigo admitted, 'but you have surrendered in all but vows.'

'There is no deception greater than self-deception, Señor' snapped Laura. 'I have no intention of marrying you, and if you're considering force, then I'll leave Spain with David.

'You are calling my bluff?' he asked softly, taking a slow step closer.

'I am! After our discussion today and your determined avowals, I see no reason to continue with this little charade.'

She brushed past him, her head held stiffly although her legs trembled and her heart was pounding like a drum, but he let her go, and it was not until she was driving with David down the long straight road to the coast that she realised how uncharacteristic his behaviour had been.

She didn't go up to David's room. After a somewhat sombre lunch when she found it impossible to talk normally, knowing that she was about to tell him she would not continue with the unofficial engagement, they sat in the quiet, empty lounge of the hotel. Here, he would not cause a scene; he was a little too civilised for that. Rodrigo would cause a scene wherever he thought it necessary, and if she had been telling him the same thing that she was telling David, then even a full lounge of interested people would not have dissuaded him from any action that came into his savage mind.

'You haven't been here two minutes,' David protested quietly when she told him. 'You can't make a decision that will affect both our lives with such speed.'

'I'm not in love with you, David. It wouldn't work, and I know you're not in love with me either. It's just a comfortable relationship.'

'I know how I feel, thanks,' he said stonily. 'Don't go making my mind up for me. My mind's been made up for too long to have you alter it with a few tidy words. We suit each other.'

'That's not being in love,' Laura said with the certainty of her feelings for Rodrigo uppermost in her mind. 'Love is like a fire. We don't feel like that.'

'You seem to be sure. You feel like that about this cold, haughty character who was with you when I came to the castle?' David asked with angry perception.

'Yes.' She couldn't deny it. There would never be anyone who could make her feel like Rodrigo made her feel. 'I couldn't marry anyone, feeling as I do.'

'You'll marry him?'

'No. He's asked me, but no.' He looked at her as if she was only confirming his opinion that she was suddenly and inexplicably mad. 'He doesn't love me,' she explained with a wistful look that stopped his anger.

'Then what's the difference?' David asked quietly, his hand covering her suddenly cold fingers. 'You're convinced that I don't love you. You know he doesn't love you. So, if nobody loves you, marry me, darling.' He was grinning and she smiled across at him, realising why this fair-haired man was her friend.

'I—I love you like a friend, David, like a brother. I love Rodrigo like a fire out of control. I'm not cheating on you or on anybody. I'm going to work out my notice and come back to England. Time and distance will do the rest. I've seen people get better from worse things than love.'

Laura rose and picked up her little white bag.

'I'd better get back. The Condesa may need me.'

'You're fond of her, aren't you?' he asked quietly, and added, 'you'll keep in touch with me?'

'Later,' she promised. 'When I've had time to settle, lick my wounds and so on.'

'I hate the bastard, you realise that?' he growled.

'I'm sorry David—I've hurt you, but you'll realise . . .'

'I'll realise that one trip to Spain has probably ruined both our lives,' he said quietly. 'But I'm not blaming you, darling. You made the decision and you're honest. If you want me for anything or if you change your mind—well, you know where I'll be.'

They stepped out of the dark of the hotel into the brilliant sunshine, and Laura stopped in wide-eyed surprise to see the familiar cream Mercedes parked at the kerb, Rodrigo leaning against it easily as if he had been there for hours.

'I'll save you the long and tiresome drive to the *castillo*, Doctor Elliott,' he said smoothly. 'As I'm here, I will drive Laura.'

She was Laura again, a pawn in a chess game, and her hand on his arm stopped David's angry growl.

'I'll go with him,' she said quietly. 'I have to go back anyway, so why not?'

'If it's all right?' he said angrily.

'It's all right.' She looked at him with affection and he suddenly took her into a bear hug, his face in her hair.

'Whenever you need me, love,' he said softly.

'I know. Goodbye, David.' She couldn't hide the tears that blinded her as she stepped into the Mercedes through the door that Rodrigo held open silently as if he were opening a cage and commanding the bird to return to captivity.

'You told him?' he asked as he slid the car into the traffic and turned for the road to the castle.

'I told him.' She held her head away, unwilling for him to see the tears that streamed down her face.

'You are upset,' he said quietly, his eyes on the road.

'Obviously! I've just ended a long and treasured friendship.'

'You told him you would marry me?' he asked with a certainty that made her temper flare over her misery, and she turned flashing blue eyes on him, brimming over with tears but sparkling with anger.

'No, I did not! I have no intention of marrying you!'

'He does not love you,' he said, looking away from her tear-wet face, his hands tight on the wheel.

'As you're the last person competent to judge what love is, I need no advice from you!' Laura snapped, turning her face deliberately away and refusing to answer when next he spoke.

The drive to the castle was conducted thereafter in silence as she nursed her pain and anger; pity for David, pity for herself and deep sadness for the Condesa finally driving anything but a slow burning anger from her mind.

She whirled from the car as they arrived and went to her room. Within five minutes she was back, storming into the study to face a sombre and silent Rodrigo and slapping down a piece of paper on the desk in front of him.

'What is this?' He stared at her in surprise, his eyes on her face, now flushed with anger.

'My resignation! I'll finish out the month and then I leave!'

'I will never let you leave me!' He was round the desk in two strides, towering over her, his hands gripping her waist with painful strength. 'If you had gone with him today, I would have followed and brought you back. Do you imagine I just happened to be outside the hotel? I was not more than a few kilometres behind you all the way. You now have no choice whatever. As you are likely to fly into a rage and leave whenever the mood takes you, you will marry me and I will have the legal right to recapture you!'

'Recapture me? You arrogant, unfeeling brute! I'm not a prize possession!'

'You are my possession, and no other man will ever touch you again. Do you not think that there was murder in my heart today when your treasured friend held you? And I have warned you before about saying that I am unfeeling.'

His mouth drove down on hers with angry delibera-tion, robbing her of breath and crushing her lips with punishing ferocity. Her struggles were utterly useless; his iron-hard arms held her fast and his anger drove him beyond anything she had imagined he would ever do.

'We will now tear up the resignation,' he ground out, looking down into her terrified face, no remorse on his when he saw her bruised and tender lips. 'The position you occupy in this castle does not allow for resignations. You are mine, and the Condesa de las Montanas does not resign!'

Any pleas she would have made, any answer she would

have given, became unnecessary as someone hammered on the door and Maria's voice, raised almost to hysteria, screamed at them from the other side of the thick oak panels.

'*Señor! Señor!*'

Rodrigo turned his head in furious amazement, his voice raised in anger.

'*Váyase!*' He was boiling with rage and it sounded clearly in his voice, but Maria did not go. Instead, her hammerings increased and her words stopped his temper in a second.

'*La Condesa! La Condesa! Señor, ella está muriendo!*'

Laura's small amount of Spanish could cope with that and, in any case, the tone of Maria's voice said it all: the Condesa was dying, and Laura was right alongside Rodrigo as he lunged for the door.

CHAPTER SEVEN

THERE was pandemonium in the Condesa's suite when they burst into the main room. The Condesa was stretched out on the same sofa where she had sat so recently talking to Laura and there were more people looking on and crying than Laura could have possibly thought would be in the castle.

As Rodrigo rushed to his mother's side, his face white and set, Laura did the first thing necessary.

'Out!' She spoke in English, but her pointing finger, her air of authority even out of uniform and their reliance on the fact that she was the only one who could do anything to help the Condesa had them leaving at once.

The Condesa was in the agonising pain of a heart attack, and no one needed to tell Laura that, she had seen it so many times before, but had never had to cope with it alone. Rodrigo was too stunned to act in any way and she realised that she was completely responsible for saving the Condesa until Miguel Hernandes arrived.

'Call the doctor!' She pushed Rodrigo aside and ripped open the Condesa's dress.

'What are you doing? Leave her to die in peace!'

'If she dies, it won't be because I've left her! Keep quiet, for God's sake, and phone Miguel!'

'He is on the way, *señorita*.' Maria's voice came from almost over her shoulder and Rodrigo turned on her.

'Go!'

'No, stay!' Laura overruled him sharply. 'I may need you, Maria. Just stay there.'

She was already pressing down hard on the Condesa's breastbone, heavy rhythmical punches that she knew would soon exhaust her. She had seen it done before, but the theory and the practice were two different things and she had seen doctors with more strength than she had exhaust themselves rapidly.

Perspiration was already beginning to run down her pale face and Rodrigo intervened.

'Let me. Tell me what to do.'

'No. Please don't speak. Just pray that Miguel gets here.'

Pushed into the background, he stared at her as if only seeing her for the first time, his eyes moving between his mother and Laura as she continued grimly with her task.

'She is blue,' he whispered, probably afraid for the first time in his life.

'I know that. If I can't force her heart into a normal beat . . .' Her own breathing was unsteady, and she found herself muttering under her breath, 'Come on, come on!'

She almost collapsed with relief as Doctor Hernandes strode into the room, his eyes taking in the scene as he came forward. Motioning them away, he took over Laura's task and, seconds later, their eyes met in understanding and thankfulness as the Condesa took a deep shuddering breath, her eyes opening and looking straight at Laura.

'Sit down, Laura,' Miguel said quietly, his eyes still on the Condesa as he listened with growing satisfaction to a heart that had returned to a steady beat.

She moved to the window to stare with unseeing eyes into the garden, and although Rodrigo moved to her side, she never looked at him. She felt she had lived through a nightmare. She had never known until a few minutes ago just how much the Condesa had come to mean to her. She had no memory of her own mother and she realised that the Condesa had so quickly filled a place in her heart that had been empty for a long time. She was shaken by what was, after all, normal routine, and it was because the whole thing had meant too much to her.

If the Condesa had died then, she would have left Rodrigo bereft. He cared for nothing but his mother; he felt almost everyone else was apart from him. It seemed that the Condesa was the only thing that kept him in the present.

'Well done, Laura. Have you ever done that before?' Miguel Hernandes was there beside them and as Rodrigo turned to his mother, the doctor signalled them both to stay where they were. She was sleeping, Maria beside her holding her hand.

'No. I've seen it done, but . . .' Laura was too tired herself to speak more, too relieved that the tall calm doctor was now in charge and the responsibility for the Condesa's life was his.

'You were quick and courageous. You did the only thing that could save her. Thank God you were here!'

He looked at the Conde with a flare of unaccustomed anger in his eyes.

'You realise that she cannot face such an attack again? I will give her now the strongest tablets she can take and hope that this will keep her alive until the operation can be done.'

'No!' Rodrigo seemed to be about to break into angry words and Laura knew that, this time, Miguel Hernandes would not back down. She intervened, too involved now to be an onlooker.

'I wish to speak to you, Señor Conde—alone, please.' Who was more surprised, Rodrigo or Miguel, she didn't know. Her own pulse threatened to race out of control at what she was about to do, but she had been quietly thinking about it since she had seen the Condesa's agonising pain, since she had realised the depths of her own involvement with the gentle smiling woman, and her mind was made up. Everything depended on how much Rodrigo really desired her and how much he needed an heir to the Montanas line.

His dark looks hovered between his mother and Laura's pale face and then he inclined his head, leading the way to his study, Laura following, her heartbeats threatening to drown the sound of her own footsteps on the mellow tiles of the hall.

He motioned her into the room ahead of him and she faced him at once as he shut the door.

'Alone and private,' he said with soft menace. 'Now, what is so urgent that I have been forced to leave my mother's side?'

'I wish to make a bargain with you.'

He stared at her in silence, a certain stillness about him that frightened her more than any angry words, and she realised that only her deep love for him prevented her from running from the room.

He was all Spaniard at this moment, closer in resemblance to the portraits that decorated the grand staircase than to the man who ran the business affairs of the family. It was impossible to imagine him flying to foreign capitals in a sleek suit, briefcase in hand, as he handled the business deals. He needed only a sword of Toledo steel with which to run her through, a change of clothes and hairstyle, and he would be more recognisable.

'You are in a position to bargain, *señorita*?'

'If the things you have said to me are true, then yes, I believe I am.'

He said nothing and she continued quickly before her courage ran out.

'You imagine that you can force me into marriage, or worse. We both know, I think, that you cannot. You've been relying on my fear and your—your . . .'

'Sexual attraction for you?' he finished for her quietly.

'I haven't put up much of a fight until today,' she admitted, her pale face flushing at his words, 'but now I will. I'm not afraid.'

'Are you not?' His piercing black eyes held hers in hypnotic stare. 'I cannot think of any time that you have not been afraid to some degree or other, in spite of your fiery temper. I find it hard to imagine that all this is suddenly changed.'

'I can return to England whenever I wish, and we both know that, too.'

'And you choose this moment to do it when there is chaos in the castle?' He stood some little distance from her, but he seemed to be towering over her, a look on his face that she had neither the time nor the courage to try to understand. What she had to say had to be said now, before her common sense rescued her.

'I wish to tell you that I will marry you, if you still want that.'

'I do.' He was so still that Laura wondered if he was breathing. Once again he appeared to be carved from stone, the brilliantly dark eyes fused with her own.

'There is a proviso. I will marry you, if you will agree to the operation that the Condesa needs.'

For a few seconds he looked at her in silence before turning to the window, his hands in his pockets as he walked away.

'You are prepared to make this sacrifice? You are so convinced of the necessity for the operation?'

'Of course I am! You saw her, she was within minutes of death!' A whirlwind of conflicting emotions raced through Laura's mind. It was no sacrifice to marry him, to have the right to be with him for the rest of her life, with or without his love.

'And if the operation fails? How will you face the consequences?' He turned his head and looked at her through narrowed eyes.

'Without it she will die, I know that. If it fails, then at least I haven't been prepared to just sit passively and wait for it to happen. I'll live with it.'

'You think I will?' There was the menace again deep in his voice, but she faced him head on.

'That is a bridge that I'll cross when I come to it, *señor*,' she said with a coldness to match his own, and she received a thin-lipped smile of admiration as he nodded.

'Very well, I agree. I need an heir, my mother likes you and after your performance today she also clearly needs you. I want you. I agree.'

'You will tell Doctor Hernandes now!' Laura demanded, wondering where all her courage was coming from, and he turned to face her with raised eyebrows.

'You are issuing orders, *señorita*?' Rodrigo enquired stiffly.

'You issued orders to me,' she replied with equal stiffness, 'and threats. I will only keep the bargain if Doctor Hernandes is informed now, before he leaves the castle.'

'You do not trust my word?' He was walking towards her and the thumping in her heart turned into thunder, but she held her ground.

'Do I have reason to? You've used your position to pressurise me. You apparently took one look at me and decided that I would do very nicely for your needs and purposes. I think you have no right to ask for my trust now or ever.'

Her cool words, delivered with no emotion, although she was close to tears as she spelled out the hurt she felt, stopped him in his tracks and he stood watching her in silence.

'It is not lack of trust, however, that makes me insist that Doctor Hernandes be informed at once. I feel that the Condesa will like to be close to the castle when she has the operation and it will take time for the necessary team to be gathered here at the hospital. Time is short. I think you know that yourself, in spite of your determination to have your own way, as usual.'

He had taken every hard word in silence, and if the lash of her tongue had reached any spot where it could hurt, he gave no sign of it. He was getting exactly what he wanted, and Laura knew that even he must now realise the need for action.

'Very well, I will inform him now.' He half turned to the door and then glanced back. 'You wish this operation to be over before the marriage?'

'No.' That surprised him, and he came back to look at her closely.

'You are not afraid that after the wedding I will change my mind and send these heart surgeons on their way?'

Laura chose to ignore the sarcastic enquiry. Her courage had now run out and she was tired, feeling the shock of the Condesa's attack, the knowledge of her promise hitting her hard. Beads of perspiration broke out on her forehead and she realised that she would soon be in a state of collapse herself if she could not rest.

'There is a risk, I know. The operation may fail, so I think she would like to see you married before she goes into hospital. She'll go in with an easier mind when she knows that the Montanas line will continue. I—I think she loved your father very much, and she will want to know that there will be another portrait one day to hang with his and your own.'

'She did love him, *señorita*. He was a very lucky man.' Rodrigo's eyes were like black pools of ice on her face and she looked away quickly. Nobody could be loved more than she loved Rodrigo.

'Then we—we should be married quickly so that she'll know that the name will continue.'

He watched her in silence for a moment, trying to read the expression on her face, but she kept her thoughts hidden from him with clouds of silvery hair, refusing to let him see anything that may be showing in her eyes.

'*Muy bien, señorita,*' he said quietly. 'I bow to your superior wisdom. I cannot promise you happiness, that is a thing too elusive to capture, but I vow that you will be honoured and protected to the best of my ability.'

He walked from the room, and Laura struggled with tears that threatened to fall. She had made a decision that she would have to live with for the rest of her life. She had promised to marry a man who did not love her, had taken it upon herself to insist on an operation that might fail, and she had no doubts as to what her life would be if it did fail. If there was any love in Rodrigo then it was for his mother and the long traditions of his ancestors and the castle. She was lucky really, she supposed, that he desired her. She wondered how long that would last.

With a resigned sigh, she went out into the hall. The milling servants had now gone and there were only two left. The castle was restored to normality, the beloved Condesa was alive.

Alfredo, the old butler, came across to her quickly, taking her hand and smiling into her eyes, tears on his lined face.

'*Bravo, señorita,*' he whispered softly. '*Muchisimas gracias.*' So, the whole castle knew about the heart attack and her struggle to save the Condesa. Laura wondered what else they knew and if one day she would have to be content with their affection when the desire that Rodrigo felt for her was burned out.

Miguel Hernandes came from the Condesa's suite and she walked quickly towards him.

'How is she?' She was dreading the reply, but he smiled at her, nodding with satisfaction.

'Sleeping. The Conde is sitting with her at the moment, but I intend to stay until much later.' He smiled at her more broadly, his eyes twinkling. 'How you managed to persuade the Conde of the necessity of the operation I do not know, but I give you my thanks. I have failed many times when trying to persuade him and have left feeling that I have been given a severe beating.' He looked quietly at her strained face. 'May I suggest that you rest? I have enough with one patient here and I do not think you look too well. Lie down for a while, or, better still, go to bed completely.'

'Will she be all right tomorrow?' asked Laura.

'Perfectly. As you saw, she was recovering before you left the suite, and I have now given her tablets which should keep her safe until we can arrange the operation.'

Laura went slowly up the great staircase. She was drained of all energy and would have welcomed Rodrigo's strong arms to carry her. She felt lonely and lost, her burst of courage over, but she knew she would have to find it again to live the rest of her life without his love. All she had was his promise that she would be honoured and protected, no doubt as befitted her title when she became the Condesa de las Montanas.

Maria was waiting for her, her normally smiling face serious and subdued, and Laura made no protest when the little maid helped her off with her dress and tucked her into bed in her slip, pulling the clothes over her and tiptoeing from the room.

It was dark when Laura opened her eyes, not knowing what had awakened her. Her mind went instantly into a flurry of guilty thoughts. How was the Condesa? Had Rodrigo told anyone of their bargain? Had she committed the unthinkable crime of missing dinner?

It was only as she swung her slender legs out of bed that she became aware that she was not alone in the room.

'Maria? Oh, why did you leave me so long?'

'It is not Maria.' Rodrigo's deep voice startled her into immobility. 'I may switch on the lamp?' He had done it before she could protest and she sat on the edge of the bed, blinking in the sudden soft light that flooded the room.

'You—you shouldn't be here.' She was terribly aware of the scanty covering of her slip but utterly incapable of throwing herself back under the covers.

'I wanted to speak to you. You are only telling me what Maria's scolding eyes have already told me. Do not worry, when our betrothal is announced, I shall not be allowed within a kilometre of you without a chaperon. Come, she has brought you one of your endless cups of tea.'

He picked up the deep blue silky robe from the chair and came towards her and, still flustered and dazed from sleep, Laura made no protest when he stood over her holding it out.

'Your tea is on the dressing-table,' he informed her quietly. 'Drink it while I talk to you.'

Securely belted in her robe, she padded on bare feet to the dressing-table, picking up her brush with unsteady fingers and running it through the untidy brightness of her hair.

'Your tea,' he repeated softly, leaning himself on the edge of the dressing-table and looking down at her with dark moody eyes.

'You ought to go,' she reminded him, looking down into the cup now clutched tightly in two hands.

'Possibly,' he agreed harshly, 'but I have little time for convention. I wish to speak to you now, not when circumstances make it appropriate. You do not need to be anxious about your reputation, it is mine that will suffer. At this moment, you are the heroine, the toast of the *castillo*. Besides,' he added, his dark face relaxing into a near smile, 'you are the no-nonsense Sister Marsh. They all know that.'

Laura couldn't find anything to say. She felt more alone and vulnerable than she had ever felt in her life. She loved this dark alarming man more strongly than she had ever imagined love could be. He was here, tearing aside conventions, calmly walking into her room as she slept, and all to discuss some point of their wedding, no doubt. The sad reality of her bargain now came clearly home to her. She had promised to marry him without any love being offered in return, she had promised to take on what would be a lifetime of responsibility, a culture that was not her own and that was as strong now as it had been in the days of his grandfather, and this she would have to face without love.

She longed to be lifted into the strong arms that were folded deliberately across his chest, to be soothed and loved. She wanted to hear his voice telling her that everything would be all right, that he loved her and they would face the frightening future together.

'There is the problem of breaking the news to my mother,' he began determinedly. 'I have no doubt that she will be delighted but, naturally, I wish to avoid any shock. I have mentioned it to Miguel Hernandes and he thinks that tomorrow would be a good time.'

'You told Miguel?' Laura looked up in surprise, a picture of wide blue eyes, silvery hair and flushed cheeks. 'What did he say?'

For a second the dark eyes surveyed her, the arrogant face relaxed, the rather cruel mouth softened.

'Sometimes you look like a child,' he observed quietly. 'Innocent, bewildered . . . What did he say? He said what I told you just now. You mean, I suppose, how did he take it?' He smiled more widely. 'A little shocked, a little disappointed, a little envious. Nothing more.'

'You've come to tell me you're going to announce it tomorrow, then?'

She looked away and he sighed impatiently.

'I have not come to tell you anything. I have come to discuss it with you. Miguel Hernandes says that it will be all right, but I want to know what you think.'

'You've never wanted to know what I think before,'

she replied, cross with him for pinning her in this embarrassing situation, aware of the eyes that constantly flickered over her, cross with herself for the feelings that were burning inside her. 'I can't see why you're starting to want my opinion now,' she added, drawing the silky robe back into place as it slipped open showing her long slender legs.

His eyes returned to her face after a sultry glance over her body.

'Now that we are to be married,' he said with quiet patience, 'you occupy a rather different position. Contrary to your beliefs, I am not a power-mad tyrant, and in this case I value your professional opinion. All major decisions will be discussed with you in future, but this decision is more yours to make than mine. I have no idea what the effect of a shock would be on her.'

'I don't know,' Laura muttered stubbornly. 'I don't want the responsibility of anything any more.'

'To be the Condesa de las Montanas is a responsibility and I know full well that you are fully capable of it,' he snapped. 'You are merely being stubborn and unco-operative. You have merely found another way to defy me.'

'You can think whatever you want!' she snapped back, her hands tightly on the cup, her eyes hidden under the clouds of her hair, and Rodrigo's uncertain temper seemed to explode.

'Stop it!' He removed the cup from her tight fingers, slamming it on the dressing-table and jerking her to her feet. 'Stop that little trick you have of hiding your face when I want to see your thoughts. Stop fighting me with everything you say, every action you take. You are to be my wife. Do you intend to fight for ever? Do you?' He shook her hard and she looked up.

She had really had more than enough for one day and

the hopelessness of her eyes, filled with tears, stopped his rage at once.

'Laura,' he murmured softly, and when he pulled her forward gently, trapping her between strong thighs, his arms closing round her, she simply came to him, softly and gladly, her face against his shoulder, her arms clinging anxiously to his neck.

'And what does this mean?' he asked quietly, his dark head against her bright hair as he cradled her gently. 'You have stopped your battles, or you are too tired to fight at the moment after your dreadful day?'

'Maybe it means that I want you as much as you say you want me,' she whispered against his chest. She was where she wanted to be, where she had wanted to be since their first alarming meeting, and his shuddering sigh thrilled her, her whole being melting against him, glorying in the quickening of his body as he recognised her surrender.

His fingers threaded through her hair as he lifted her head to search her face with eyes already hot with passion.

'You could not want me that much,' he whispered softly. 'You could never stand it. You are not as strong as I.'

For seconds he stared into her eyes until her own eyes closed, unable to face the burning need they saw, and then he pulled her fiercely against him, his thighs trapping her slender hips, his hands holding her in powerful possession.

'*Te quiero*', he groaned. '*Te quiero!*'

A shudder ran through the magnificent length of him, and Laura felt already possessed as her softness yielded to the hard planes of his body and his mouth covered hers in an agony of desire.

All pretence ended, she wound her arms around his neck with the same fierce desire that he showed, going where he led, every inch of her willing and yielding as his kisses deepened into a frenzy of passion.

'You are everything I imagined,' he gasped against her lips, 'perfection. Every part of you designed in heaven for me.'

She could see no reason to hold back. She was going to be his wife, she loved him and wanted him with with a fire that almost matched his own, and her eager lips returned his kisses as fire grew between them, a conflagration held down since their first meeting, desire arching from one to the other like the lightning over the mountains.

The silken robe proved no barrier to his urgent hands, and Laura gasped with pleasure as the strong warmth of his fingers slid beneath the lacy top of her slip to caress the fullness of breasts that surged readily into his strong hands.

'Soft and innocent from sleep,' murmured Rodrigo against the arch of her neck, his lips wandering down its silken length to find the warm soft curves that his hands possessed. 'Did I catch you at some vulnerable time, *encantadora*, or is this the end of your struggles?'

He raised his glossy dark head, his eyes devouring her, his mouth claiming hers again when she moaned in protest and searched eagerly for his lips.

His hands were discovering the slenderness of her waist, the smooth length of her hips, the deep curves of her breasts, his lips returning to hers again and again in ever-increasing demand.

'Do you know what will happen when our betrothal is announced?' he whispered into her hair when their hearts were beating together like the thunder of drums and his hands were tightly on her hips, impelling her into closer contact. 'Tradition will stifle us. I will hardly see you. Here in the *castillo*, time will run back to my grandfather's days and I will not be allowed so much as to touch your hand until our wedding night. Must I wait so long before you belong to to me? Come with me now, let me spend the night with your beauty in my arms.'

'I can't! I—I . . .'

Laura's protests were stopped by lips that devoured her and then he buried his face in her hair.

'You mean that you will not,' he groaned. 'You are still afraid, burning in need but still afraid to come to me. Your stubborn little mind has still not surrendered.'

She expected anger, but there was no anger on his face when he raised his head and looked down at her, only a rueful acceptance.

'I think that today has been too much for your disciplined coolness, Laura,' he observed softly, fastening her securely into her robe. 'And waking you from sleep, I have caught you off balance. It was well worth it.' He tipped up the face she would have hidden from him. 'Come, we are too involved, you and I, for any hiding from me. We now know something that is very definite. We are both burned by the same flame. For good or ill, we need each other. Therefore the wedding must be arranged speedily for our sakes as well as for my mother.'

Laura suddenly buried her hot face against his chest, not wanting him to go, wanting to cling on to the magic that he wove around her. Not one word of love, but more desire than any woman could hope for in a lifetime. This man might bring her heartache, had brought it already, but she loved him with a fierce passion that weeks before she would have thought impossible.

'What is it?' he whispered against her hair, holding her tightly against him.

'Nothing.' She shook her head against the smooth silk of his shirt, suddenly looking up as an idea occurred to her. 'Have I missed dinner?'

He laughed aloud, cupping her face between his hands and looking into her eyes.

'You are a delight to me—do you know that? You scold me, fight me, surrender like a flame in my arms and then, like a child, you are hungry!' He stood and lifted her away. 'If you will not come to me, then I will place you in a less vulnerable position. As to your dinner—yes, you have missed it. Miguel and I took ours in my study. There was neither time nor inclination for a formal meal tonight and Eduardo, as you know, is away again.'

'What about Carlota?'

'She ate in her room, I believe. She is, I think, sulking. Her nose is slightly pushed out by your praises that are being sung around the *castillo*.' Rodrigo smiled teasingly into her eyes. 'You are jealous?'

'Yes!' Laura looked at him with her old defiance. She had promised to marry him, but she would not put up with lady friends once the marriage had taken place and he might as well know it.

'*Bueno!* We progress!' She could see a glint of amusement in his eyes and she gave him a blue-eyed glare.

'When we're married, Rodrigo . . .'

'You will sleep in my bed,' he cut in determinedly. 'Have I asked for more, my fiery one? You think I need more than one woman? Believe me, you will occupy all my nights and many of my days. The only thing you need to be jealous of is the fact that you will have little free time and almost no sleep.'

He trailed his fingers down her flushed cheeks and then, quite unexpectedly, he kissed her hand.

'I will see you tomorrow, Laura, as you refuse to see me tonight. Maria will bring you a tray, and do not worry about my mother, her maid is with her, she is sleeping quietly and Miguel will return in two hours to check on her. He has ordered that you sleep until morning.'

'Why didn't you leave me sleeping, then?' she enquired tartly, determined to get the last word in.

'I intended to.' He looked at her with regretful
amusement. 'But I began to think of our wedding and,
from there, my mind naturally turned to my bed. *Hasta
mañana*, Laura. Sleep well.'

Not much chance of that, she thought frustratedly, still
dazed from the heat of his kisses. She was still standing
wistfully where he had left her when Maria came in with
her tray, a glass of champagne standing amongst the
sparkle of silver.

'Why did you bring me champagne at this time of
night?' Laura asked in astonishment.

'Oh, it is *El Conde, señorita*,' Maria explained with a
shrug of dismissal. 'He said to tell you that it would help
you sleep after all your excitement. I expect it is a good
idea. You must still feel excited that you saved the
Condesa and that she is to have her operation.'

'Oh, I do, I do,' Laura answered quietly, turning her
rosy face away. Rodrigo had not meant that at all; he did
well to compare himself with the devil.

CHAPTER EIGHT

EVEN though Laura was up and about very early, she never saw Rodrigo the following morning. Apparently he had left the castle as soon as it was light to make the long trip to Córdoba—to join Eduardo, no doubt, she thought. Carlota at any rate, had been left behind, and she wondered rather anxiously how long it would be before that particular nuisance would be leaving.

The glowering face of the Spanish girl seemed to be everywhere she looked, and Laura was glad to be with the Condesa for the whole of the morning and the better part of the afternoon, taking her lunch in the Condesa's suite and feeling great relief that the Condesa seemed to be almost back to normal.

The subject of the operation was a great source of conversation. The Condesa wanted to know everything and, with the help of Miguel Hernandes, it was explained. Laura imagined he would mention her impending marriage when they had a word in private, but he did not. Apparently Spanish courtesy made him hold his tongue and whatever he thought about the sudden permission that had been given for the operation, and the equally sudden announcement to him by Rodrigo that they intended to marry, he kept to himself.

It was clear that the Condesa was glad the operation was to go ahead and also clear that she realised who she could thank for this change of mind on her son's part.

'I knew from the start that you'd made a great impression on him, Laura. I only hope that when he marries he chooses someone who can calm his temper

and talk a little sense. I doubt if he's going to find that
with Señorita Martinez.'

'I—I shouldn't worry about that,' Laura said quietly,
longing to tell the Condesa and put her mind at rest. But
still, they were a very noble family; perhaps the Condesa
would not be as taken with the idea as Rodrigo thought.
She did not know anything about Carlota's background,
but from her haughty manner and her costly clothes, she
would probably have been more acceptable if the
Condesa had liked her.

Many times she found the Condesa watching her
closely and, when the Condesa had settled down for her
mid-afternoon nap, her maid sitting with her ever-
present knitting beside the bed to watch her with sharp
anxious eyes, Laura was glad to escape. She did not like
subterfuge and the grey eyes of the Condesa could be as
penetrating as the night-black eyes of her son.

With Doctor Hernandes constantly in and out of the
castle she had felt it necessary to wear her uniform today,
and she was thankful, once in the quiet of her room, to
fling her white cap on to the dressing-table and drop
down on to the bed for a brief rest. Underhand behaviour
was quite exhausting, she thought ruefully, and she
determined to speak to Rodrigo the moment he came
back, a little sigh of dismay, leaving her as she reminded
herself of the long drive to Córdoba. Maybe he wouldn't
be back today after all.

That little worry was cleared up rapidly, however, as
the door opened and Maria came staggering in, her face
almost hidden behind piles of boxes, her expression
hovering between glee and amazement. Rodrigo followed, also weighed down.

'On the bed, Maria,' he ordered. 'We will surround the
señorita with these goodies like a toy castle, eh?'

Maria did exactly as he ordered and left the room,

giggling with maddening joy as Laura sat up in the middle of the wave of disorder that had suddenly struck her comfortable tidy bed.

'You've finally gone completely mad!' she laughed with a familiarity that the day before would have been unthinkable, kneeling in the middle of the chaos and looking with bewilderment at the array of boxes of different sizes and shapes that surrounded her. 'Well, what is all this?'

Rodrigo was leaning against the door, so different from the man she had found so alarming when she first met him that her heart almost stopped with love.

'When we are married,' he said softly, his eyes on her deep blue uniform, 'I think I will have that starchy little number mounted in the great hall with the other relics of battle.' He eased himself upright and wandered over to her, looking down into her face with a glint of devilment in his eyes. 'The boxes? Your new clothes. I should have gone to Seville, but it was too far. We will go there together later.'

The blow hit Laura harder than she could have imagined, like the blow of a hammer, the animation dying from her face as she remembered how she had addressed him with such familiarity as he had entered the room, her thoughts as she had spoken to the Condesa running through her head simultaneously. Carlota would have been more suitable if the Condesa had liked her. Rodrigo was trying to make her more acceptable. The prince and the kitchenmaid.

She felt inadequate, totally out of her depth, suddenly aware as she had never been in her life of her own lowly beginnings, her own lifestyle in England. She was light years away from Rodrigo, she had no idea how to be a Condesa, no idea how to cope with the running of a castle—so many servants.

The clothes were a first step in a re-education programme. She would be moulded into a different being, her own personality trapped like a bird inside. Rodrigo had even chosen them himself, perfectly certain no doubt that her choice would have been tasteless and unsuitable.

'I have never given clothes to a woman before,' he said quietly, watching her with dark unreadable eyes, 'but I would have imagined that any woman would have been, by now, tearing the wrapping off to look into the boxes like someone given freedom of choice in Aladdin's Cave.'

'It's very nice of you, *señor*, but I can't accept any of them,' Laura said stiffly, still kneeling, hands clenched tightly in her lap.

She gave a gasp of alarm as his hands came tightly round her waist and she was lifted into the air to be held above the ground as he looked up into her eyes. The precarious position forced her to put her hands on his shoulders and he slid her deliberately down the length of his body before clamping her fast in his arms.

'*Señor?*' he queried softly. 'You greeted me as I came in as you would greet your lover, and now I am *señor*? You have jumped back with hasty feet into your fortress because I have driven like a fiend to Córdoba, faced the heat of the day and driven back to be with you for a while before our betrothal is announced and tradition separates us? For this feat of devotion I am to be closed out of your life as you slam your fortress door?'

'I—I've said it was nice of you,' she muttered, hiding her face.

'It was more than nice,' he snapped irritably, jerking her head up with impatient fingers. 'It is probably the insanity that you diagnosed! I expected to please you, but obviously nothing I do will ever meet with your approval.

Most men would expect the sweetness of the cake after such effort and devotion; I get the frost of the icing!'

'I've hurt you,' Laura whispered regretfully.

'I cannot say that I feel deliriously happy,' he grated, his eyes beginning to glow with the anger she hated.

'I—I know I'm unsuitable to be the next Condesa de las Montanas,' she began slowly, afraid to make matters worse. 'I know that you're only trying to see that I fit in properly, but I feel inadequate already without you rushing to alter me so soon. I—I know I'll have to change, to be someone who looks more the part,' she looked up at him with anxious eyes. 'I won't let you down. I'll be very careful, but I can't do it all at once.' Her eyes slid sideways to the piles of boxes, boxes she was afraid to open. 'I can't go from being just me to being what you expect all in one day.'

She looked up at him again, expecting to see tight-lipped arrogance, but the hard grip on her relaxed almost to tenderness and Rodrigo was looking at her with astonishment.

'This is what you believe?' he asked incredulously. 'You think that I seek to change you?' His hand came to her face, holding it up to his dark, imperious gaze. He was utterly aristocratic, the Conde de las Montanas, and his next words astonished her in her turn. 'I expect you to remain as you are, Laura. I demand it! I do not want some glossy creature polished for the part. My desires are wrapped around you, not some unseen glittering beauty that you feel you should become.' He was looking at her intently and she was staring back with wide blue eyes.

'If you feel inadequate, then it is high time that I began to protect you as I promised. It is time that I showed you that you are more than adequate for my life. As to the clothes, you have complained that you brought only things to use in your work. I sought only to please you as your desire last night pleased me. They are merely a gift, one final act before we are separated by tradition.

'I'm sorry.' Her fingers were anxiously pleating the red silk of his tie and he stroked back her hair.

'You will accept them?' he asked. 'You will open the boxes and be happy as any woman with new clothes and lots of presents to open?'

Laura nodded and then looked up, her eyes shining, her soft lips tilted in a smile.

'Yes. Thank you, Rodrigo.'

He looked at her intently, his eyes beginning to glow with a light that was not anger, and Laura felt a shiver of pleasure race along her nerve endings as his body moved restlessly closer, his arms tightening. For seconds they looked at each other in silence, unsmiling, fire beginning to burn between them, and Rodrigo tilted her face up to his with strong possessive fingers.

'Kiss me!' he ordered sharply. 'Kiss me, Laura!'

She had never been the one to instigate any passion between them, and she felt a thrill of alarm at the sharp command in his voice, but it was only what she wanted to do, only what she had been silently begging from him as they looked at each other, and she wound her arms around his neck, standing on tiptoe to press her lips to his.

He made no response; worse, his arms fell away. Only his hands touched her, lightly gripping her waist. She kissed him more urgently, demanding a response, bereft that there was no answering warmth, her arms tightening, her body fighting to get closer as the deceptively light grip on her waist held her away from him.

He never moved until her kisses were feverish with desperation, until her little moans of protest had grown into a continuous murmur of distress, and then his hands moved against her, running from her waist to capture and mould her breasts, moving to the base of her spine to pull her hard against him as his mouth opened over hers.

Already driven to a frenzy of excitement by her own urgency, Laura gasped against his mouth as he took control of her trembling body, his tongue running round the inner softness of her lips, his hands compelling her to accept the evidence of his desire.

Suddenly he lifted her, placing her urgently on the bed, his arm sweeping aside the boxes as he came down with her, his body covering her own.

Laura was incapable of speech, swept into a rapture of desire by the strength of the masculine body that moved impatiently over hers, arching against him as his fingers dealt with the buttons of her dress before unclipping the neat, dark belt to toss it aside.

She heard his gasp of pleasure as his hands encountered no further barriers and moved with ruthless determination to the swollen curves of her breasts.

'Rodrigo!' Laura moaned with pain and pleasure as his lips left hers to seek the excitement his hands had uncovered, his teeth nipping her satin-smooth skin, his tongue soothing the hurt. She was shaking with excitement as his kisses trailed from one rose-tipped breast to the other, pausing to allow the tip of his tongue to weave a pattern of fire through the deep valley between to the pulsating softness of her stomach, breathing in the scent of her skin.

Throbbing with her own passion, she was mindless of his presumption, willing to be dominated by the dark, silent being who had skilfully forced her to yield. But when his hands slid possessively over her slender legs to the smooth curve of her thighs, she gasped with alarm, struggling free to sit up breathless and shaken, her face still flushed with excitement, her mounting fright stilled as she found his eyes laughing into hers, a lightheartedness in him that she had never seen before, tempering his desire.

'I almost pulled you from your fortress, *querida*,' he laughed, his breathing still uneven as he reached for her, pulling her to her feet, the swift silent attack over, his fingers fastening the buttons they had parted. 'You still imagine that you are unsuitable for me? I would marry you in that starchy uniform if it was the only way that you would come to me, and the world could think whatever it chose. When we are together there will be no world; there will be only desire and fulfilment. I will know only how much I want you.'

'You almost tore my dress,' she murmured shakily, her head still on his shoulder, her body reluctant to leave the hands that still moved seductively and slowly over her.

'There are others in the boxes,' he said with cool unconcern, 'and others to buy in Seville if I should tear them all. Come, choose a dress for dinner. Tonight we announce our betrothal and the dress you are wearing is badly crumpled.'

Laura blushed hotly as she met his teasing eyes and he looked at her quizzically for a second, his head tilted back speculatively.

'Your face often flushes like a rose, sometimes in anger, but more often when I look at you; strange for someone who feels so much desire. It will be unusual to be the lover of one with such tender feelings, with so much deep shyness.' Her eyes fell beneath the probing dark gaze, a gaze from which the laughter had fled. 'What do you feel I wonder, Laura? What thoughts race through that clever little mind?' He lifted her face with suddenly hard fingers, enclosing her head with strong hands, forcing her eyes to meet his. 'One day, you will lie in my arms and tell me everything that I wish to know. One day, I will be so completely your lover that you will confess everything that is deep within your soul. Until then, I will wait content that I have you in my possession, even if your mind is still your own.'

She pulled free, grabbing her robe and fleeing to the sanctuary of the bathroom, painfully aware that his words had never mentioned love, that he was only filled with desire and the urge to own her. He had not even called himself her husband when he had been considering the future. He would be her lover and nothing more. He made his own laws and she had no doubt that when they were married he would make hers, too.

Soothed from the warm bath, the stinging excitement quelled and the later hurt lessened, she returned to her bedroom, to find Maria hovering with barely suppressed indignation over the scattered boxes, her eyes on the untidy bed.

'You have not opened the parcels, *señorita*,' she accused, her eyes clearly asking what other events had been occupying her time.

'I was too tired, Maria,' Laura improvised with an arrogance to match Rodrigo's. She was going to rule this *castillo*; she might as well begin now to copy the conduct of her lord and master. 'I know what's in the boxes. You can help me in a minute.'

It worked so well that she almost spoiled it all by laughing. Maria's attitude changed at once and she began to tidy the bed with a happy little smile on her face, her anxiety eased completely by Laura's nonchalant manner. But she stopped quickly, her surprise equalling Laura's when the door opened and, without any preliminary knock or word of excuse, Carlota Martinez walked quickly into the room.

'I wish to speak to Sister Marsh—alone!' she announced with sharp impatience. 'Leave us!'

There was no doubt that this was not to be a quiet,

friendly chat, and Maria hesitated, glancing at Laura for confirmation, a thing that only incensed Carlota further.

'Leave us! You will be called when you are needed!'

'It's all right, Maria.' Laura's quiet voice and easy manner somewhat satisfied the startled little maid, but she left only slowly and Carlota was in too much of a rage to wait for the door to close before she began.

'I can see that Rodrigo has been buying you presents,' she snapped. 'Is it for your efforts on behalf of his mother or for your services to him?'

'What exactly do you mean by that?' Laura was quietly furious at the arrogance of the Spanish girl and the implications of her remarks.

'I should think it obvious! I saw Rodrigo come in here with that half-witted maid and I saw her leave. I also saw him leave, a good deal later.' Carlota's face was dark with fury. 'I have no doubt that you are a passing desire to him. I'm quite accustomed to that, but his paramours do not normally live in the same house.'

'I think you had better leave my room, Señorita Martinez.' Laura's own rage was growing by the minute, but the girl ignored it.

'And I think you had better leave Spain, Sister Marsh! Your services will not be needed when the Conde and I are married. The Condesa Helen will not need a nurse; she will be well, or in a suitable nursing home.'

'You are quite sure, *señorita*, that the Conde intends to marry you?' Laura asked quietly. To say that the words had been a shock to her was a great understatement, but her mind refused to believe it. She knew that Rodrigo would not permit the cruel future that this girl had mapped out for the Condesa. Carlota would be the the most monstrous daughter-in-law that any one could have, and it was impossible even to begin to imagine that Rodrigo had intended to marry her.

Laura was quite sure that any love he had was for the delicate woman who now awaited her operation. Carlota's attitude to the Condesa was so very obvious that there was no way that Rodrigo would have thought of marrying her.

'We have talked of the future quite often lately and the Conde said nothing of his plans to marry you,' Laura said flatly. 'I imagine you're telling me this just to make trouble.'

'Naturally he said nothing. He enjoys having a mistress, one who was probably more than willing not more than an hour ago. The Conde and I are already engaged. We are keeping the matter secret until his mother can be told at an appropriate time. You have noticed surely how that woman dislikes me? Her health is a constant nuisance; naturally we cannot tell her yet. When this operation is over, however, she will have to face the truth.'

Laura's sceptical expression seemed to cause Carlota no embarrassment; in fact she seemed amused.

'The ring, Sister Marsh!' She drew a gold chain from beneath the neck of her dress, a beautiful diamond ring attached, and her eyes were triumphant and satisfied at the shock on Laura's face. 'As I said, it is a secret, but I will not have Rodrigo taking a mistress under my very nose. The Condesa will be told unless I have your assurance that you intend to leave the *castillo*.'

Laura was still standing silently, her eyes unbelieving, when the door opened again and Rodrigo strode into the room, closely followed by a defiant looking Maria.

'Forgive me that I did not knock, Laura, but Maria felt that you might need assistance, although I have little doubt that you can handle any situation.'

His dark eyes were searching her face, and what he

saw there did nothing to soften his expression as he turned to Carlota.

'What are you doing in Señorita Marsh's room?' The biting tones held no politeness, and Carlota faced him with reddened cheeks, her arrogance greatly diluted.

'Merely visiting, Rodrigo.' She smiled with alluring red lips, but there was no answering smile.

'Then perhaps we can call your visit over? We will see you at dinner. Show Señorita Martinez out, Maria, and wait outside!'

He was daunting, the master of the *castillo*, and Laura wondered how she could tell him. He clearly had no idea that Carlota had already shown her the ring. He didn't even seem to care what the girl thought. His eyes never left Laura's face as the two of them left the room and the door closed quietly.

'What has she been saying to you?' he demanded, no longer the exciting being who had made love to her but a dark, towering alien. 'And do not think of protecting her from my anger. I wish to know why someone who has never even had the courtesy to speak to you should suddenly need to have a cosy chat and send Maria out.'

Laura was startled that he had noticed Carlota's constant ignoring of her, her heart lifting a little that it had clearly annoyed him, although he said nothing—but there was the ring.

'She came to tell me that she was engaged to you.' She looked straight at him, dreading the moment when he would confirm it.

'And you believed it, of course,' he snapped. 'Naturally I intend to marry two women. It would be normal for someone who in your eyes is such a barbarian!'

'No, I didn't believe it!' she snapped back, her eyes sparkling with anger and suppressed tears. 'Although I did have a few misgivings when she showed me the ring.'

His eyes narrowed to a glittering blackness.

'So! You have seen the famous betrothal ring of the Montanas?' Each word seemed to hit her like a shockwave and the tears threatened to choke her.

'So it seems.' Laura turned away, but Rodrigo spun her back to face him.

'Describe it!'

'You know it as well as I do! It's a huge showy diamond!' One tear escaped her eyes and trickled slowly down her pale cheek, and his eyes followed it with a look of astonishment but his temper did not lessen.

'And what if I were to tell you that I do not have the right to produce the betrothal ring of my family? By tradition the ring is held in safe keeping by the Condesa since it was first brought to the *castillo* generations ago. The betrothal ring of the Montanas is an emerald, its setting old and exquisite. The ring may be showy,' he added angrily, his eyes leaving the slow and relentless progress of her tears down her face to return to her eyes, 'but it is also priceless!'

Laura was stunned, waiting for his anger to really hit her, to be poured on her that she had no faith, but he carried on, ignoring the growing volume of her steady tears.

'The ring will be yours only until you produce an heir to the *castillo*, and then it will be your duty to keep it until it is needed for our son's betrothal. When you give me a son, then I will give you diamonds, as is also the custom. This time there will be a break in tradition, however— the diamonds will be surrounded with sapphires to match your doubting, angry eyes!'

Her eyes were not angry at the moment, they were drenched in tears, tears that silently fell and refused to stop, but Rodrigo ingored that.

'You have little faith in my word it seems if you will

allow any mad woman to sway your judgement.'

'Perhaps I would be able to face things like that more easily if I fitted in here more readily,' she said quietly. 'Carlota's probably more your type, more the sort of person who . . .'

'Enough of this nonsense!'He pulled her into his arms and looked down at her face. 'Tears! I have seen you cry only once and that partly in anger: tears for your lost friend. Why do you cry now, *amiga*? You are thinking perhaps that Carlota and I are lovers and that is why she feels secure enough to invent lies to distress you? Well, we are not and never have been lovers.'

'Then why is she here?' Laura tried to turn her face away; she rarely cried and she couldn't face the thought of being made to stand there while Rodrigo watched her tears so calmly.

'Her father was an old friend of my father. She has been coming here since she was a child and staying very rarely since she has grown into a spoiled and slightly odd virago. I kept her around this time to make you jealous, and all I succeeded in doing was alarming my mother, because until this moment you have been more than capable of dealing with Carlota and have shown no trace of the jealousy that I wanted to see.' He was growling at her quietly, angrily, and it annoyed her. What had he got to be angry about?

'Well, she can go! She said she didn't want you to have a mistress and neither do I, and I'm warning you, Rodrigo, that if . . .'

She suddenly stopped, stunned to see that his face had relaxed into a wide grin.

'Ah, little fiery dragon, your jealousy is showing at last!' His hands gently wiped the tears from her soft cheeks and his eyes met hers with gleaming satisfaction. 'Now I can wipe away your tears, now I can love you better. That is what you want, is it not?'

His lips captured her trembling mouth, soothing and calming as his hands stroked the tension out of her spine.

'*Tranquilo*,' he whispered softly against her lips. 'From this moment I will let nothing hurt you. After tonight you will wear the emeralds of the Montanas and you will be secure and honoured. Your future will be written into the very fabric of the *castillo*, and soon you will give me a son to carry the name of my ancestors into the future. I will wait patiently to possess you. I will never alarm you again. I have what I want, your tears and your trembling body tell me.'

He held her away from him, looking deeply into her eyes, pride and satisfaction on his face, before he left her abruptly and went to call Maria into the room, beaming at the slightly rebellious figure who had been standing as close to the door as she could get.

'You have my thanks for alerting me to the fact that Señorita Martinez was in the room. I can see that when I chose you to guard my *novia*, I chose well.'

Maria's face was a picture of astonishment and joy.

'No doubt the whole of the *castillo* will be overjoyed that the next Condesa de las Montanas will also be an *inglesa*. I know that she already commands their affection. I have not overlooked the fact either that your loyalty to the Señorita Laura has given you the courage to defy me.'

Maria's face flooded with colour, but he merely laughed.

'Do not worry. Your duty to her overrides all others, and I am pleased. So pleased in fact that I will tell you that you are the first to know of our betrothal; you know even before the Condesa. Now, prepare the *señorita* for dinner and then you may pass the word around the *castillo*, as you are no doubt wishing to do. The betrothal will take place before we dine. You know what to do?'

'*Si*, Señor Conde!'

Maria bustled forward and began to attack the boxes of dresses, and Rodrigo turned for one look at Laura. There was an air of angry determination about him that brought a slight shiver of alarm to her, although she knew that his anger was directed at Carlota. She felt, too, a moment of panic that her future was now firmly settled. Clearly he intended to stand for no further nonsense, no further delay, and she could only hope that the Condesa would take the matter with the same delight that had shown on Maria's face.

Rodrigo was waiting in the great hall as Laura descended the stairs. The soft folds of the blue chiffon dress she had chosen from the many expensive dresses in the boxes whispered around her slim ankles and the look in her eyes must have been very clear, because he stepped forward and took her hand.

'Come,' he said in a softly reassuring voice. 'You are quite beautiful and everything will be all right. From this night, the protection of the *castillo* will close around you until I hold you safely in my arms on our wedding night.'

The words were so beautiful, so much what she wanted to hear, that they brought a glow to her face that remained there as he opened the door to the *sala* where the others awaited dinner.

The formality of the entrance brought the Condesa to her feet, a flicker of some great emotion at the back of her eyes.

'*Madrecita*,' Rodrigo said with an almost courtly formality. 'I wish to present to you Señorita Laura Marsh, who has consented to be my wife.'

The Condesa gave a little gasp, and Laura watched her with twofold anxiety. There was the very real danger of a shock, and there was also the great possibility that she would disapprove. To be fond of Laura as a nurse and companion was in no way equal to welcoming her as a daughter-in-law and the next Condesa de las Montanas. She knew of Laura's quiet and ordinary upbringing.

For a second she said nothing, and then she stepped forward and hugged Laura with more strength than anyone could have imagined her to have.

'My last worries are over! I think he has met his match,' she said, for Laura's ears alone. 'Make him happy, Laura.'

If only she could! She turned her head and looked up at Rodrigo and his hand came to her shoulder in an action that was both protective and possessive. He never even looked down at her—his eyes were meeting the smiling gaze of Eduardo, a look of amused understanding passing between them, but he had felt her eyes on him and reacted instantly. The protection he had promised was around her.

Eduardo's approval was very obvious as he came to kiss her hand and it was almost as if she had suddenly found a brother, but Carlota stayed where she was, her face pale and tight.

'Come, Carlota,' Rodrigo said with quiet menace.' You have not wished us well. It is fortunate that you have been here these past few days. Now that you have witnessed my betrothal you will be able to leave us with an easy mind.'

His subtle words were not lost on anyone, least of all on the flustered girl, who came forward with obvious reluctance. He was inviting her to leave with all possible speed, and Laura hoped she would never have to face the jealous eyes of the Spanish girl again after tonight.

'I will be invited to the wedding, Rodrigo?' Carlota smiled but her eyes were cold and angry.

'Naturally,' he said with smooth, cold ease. 'It would

be very strange if you were not. Your father was my own father's dearest friend and, in any case, I imagine that you will wish to see my marriage to Laura.'

There was a small thrill of fear in Laura that even Rodrigo's protective hand could not prevent and she needed a very determined effort to push the fear to the back of her mind. She knew that his protection would always be around her, but her reaction to Carlota was as instinctive as any wild animal. There was a dangerous anger inside the girl that would never go. Rodrigo had said that she was slightly odd, and Laura could see that clearly at this moment. The black eyes were staring and icy cold, although the red lips smiled and smiled. It brought a shiver to Laura, and Rodrigo's arm came round her quickly and firmly, drawing her close to his side, the power of his own displeasure turning Carlota's gaze away from the girl who had become so quickly the most loved in the Castle of Fire next to the Condesa.

The Condesa had disappeared and, in a few minutes, Rodrigo led Laura into the great hall, taking her hand and walking to the long table that held the glowing arrangements of flowers. The Condesa waited there and every servant in the *castillo* was gathered round, more staff than she imagined could exist in one place. The stood in a huge circle around the hall, their glasses charged with champagne, their eyes bright and happy, waiting for a glimpse of the girl who would marry the Conde.

The box that held the ring was old, old enough to have been the original container for the magnificent emerald that the Condesa lifted from it and handed to her son. He took Laura's hand with steady fingers, his eyes guarded and lowered as he slid the heavy ring on to her finger.

She looked up at him and he raised his head slowly, his eyes meeting hers, and for a second she saw an emotion

in the dark eyes that almost stopped her heart. It was a
mere flicker, but for that moment they seemed to be
alone in the vast hall.

His strong hand closed around her fingers, enclosing
the ring and her slender hand in one all-encompassing
and possessive grasp as he looked deeply into her eyes,
his face still and tight.

'You are mine,' he said with a softness that kept the
words to her ears alone. 'At last, you wear the ring and I
will never let you go. Leave me and I will follow and kill
you.'

He raised her hand in the air and the alarming spell
was broken as the Condesa announced,

'The betrothal of Rodrigo Estéban Diaz, Conde de las
Montanas!'

'*Viva! Viva!*' The great shout went up around the hall
as it had done for countless generations as all glasses were
raised and Rodrigo kissed Laura's hand.

She was led around the hall and introduced to each
person in turn, names that would take her months to
learn, but her hand was still firmly in Rodrigo's and she
felt a great burst of happiness that drowned all other
fears, realising that now nothing could separate her from
the man who moved at her side, his eyes now smiling, the
vibrant and strange emotion gone as he looked down at
her.

'I feel like a princess,' she whispered shakily, in awe
that she was the centre of all this tradition and ceremony.

'You look for once totally vulnerable,' he murmured.
'And I would take you and calm your fears in my arms,
but Maria is now prepared for her role and from this
moment, until our wedding, her whims will rule my life,
and yours, whether you stay a sharp little dragon or
become a timid little dove.'

'What do you mean?' Laura looked across at Maria,

who was at the centre of an animated group of women servants, their chatter determined and vigorous.

'I chose her to guard you,' Rodrigo smiled wickedly, 'and I knew that she would. She is now not so much your servant as your *dueña*. I am thankful that there is an excuse to hurry the wedding, or the looks that we are getting would be scandalised as they wondered why there is to be an almost indecent haste!'

Laura blushed prettily and felt a twinge of alarm as she met the small, dark, determined eyes of Maria, but his fingers trailed secretly on the sensitive skin of her arm and her happiness was almost complete.

Many people through the ages had married for expediency, and as she looked around the towering height of the hall, she realised that here, too, this ceremony must have been performed between people who were in no way in love. They could not all have ended in unhappiness. Perhaps with the coming of children Rodrigo would look on her differently, perhaps one day he would look at her with love as well as desire.

CHAPTER NINE

THE guests began to gather for the wedding: distant relatives, old friends, people that Laura had never met and would rarely meet again. Almost every room in the *castillo* was filled and the Condesa rarely left her suite as she wisely conserved her strength for the tasks that would befall her as the mother of the Conde.

The traditional preparations were easy to follow, so that much of the work could be delegated to others, and as Laura was not to be allowed to help, she spent most of her time talking to the Condesa, although she could not confide in her any of her fears and heartaches.

The days dragged by with leaden repetitiveness and she saw little of Rodrigo except at dinner, when the grand dining-room was filled to overflowing with guests.

It seemed that he was right, tradition dictated everything, and Maria now seemed to have changed from a defending tigress to a dangerous dragon who watched her closely and followed her around like a *dueña*. Laura felt that if she so much as glanced sideways at Rodrigo she would be scolded.

She learned that the Montanas brides entered the great cathedral alone, with no supporting arm to lean on, and she was not terribly amused when Eduardo told her that in his opinion it was because in the days of Rodrigo's ancestors, the bride had probably been kidnapped and would have no male member of her family to support her down the aisle. The betrothed of the Montanas came alone, their walk down the long aisle of the cathedral lonely and virginal as a nun, and she shivered at the idea.

157

The rather grand preparations that were taking place began to unnerve her again and she was filled with plenty of misgivings, plenty of feelings of inadequacy. It was something that she had to face without Rodrigo, because she now saw more of Eduardo than she did of her future husband. Rodrigo was distant and aloof to such an extent that she wondered if he now regretted his impetuosity in agreeing to her bargain. He sat as far away as possible from her at dinner, his only remarks polite and brief, until she began to feel utterly forlorn.

She took to walking alone in the gardens, but even this delight was spoiled by the fact that she worried about leaving the Condesa. There would be no honeymoon for the present. Neither of them felt able to leave the Condesa and Laura spent much of her time watching her anxiously. She knew from Miguel that the team would be gathered in the little hospital by the day of the wedding and that all that would remain then was to trust to their skills.

The day before the wedding there had been a rehearsal in the cathedral. The Condesa had not undertaken the long drive, so that it was only Rodrigo who had noticed the tight fear on Laura's face as she had stepped from Eduardo's car on their return to the *castillo*. She had eaten no lunch and had even found it necessary to escape from her room, being unable to bear the chatter and excitement of Maria for one second longer.

It was soothing to be in the walled garden, but her relief was shortlived as the sight of Rodrigo in front of her brought her to a startled halt. Clearly he too had decided to walk alone and he would accuse her of waylaying him and breaking the long traditions of his family.

Laura turned to leave, but he was beside her with his

usual silent speed, taking her arm firmly and turning her to him as he raised eyes that mirrored her anxiety.

'Come to me!' he ordered in a voice that contained very little tenderness. 'Fight me and rage at me, but never be afraid.'

'What—what about the traditions?'

'The devil take the traditions!' he rasped, pulling her into his arms. 'I only need to know that you will never go, that you will never leave me, that you will have the courage to stay with me in spite of all the things that are alien to you.'

There was a fierce light in his eyes that puzzled her, and his attitude was not at all encouraging.

'We're not supposed to meet alone,' she reminded him a little uneasily, and his face darkened with a burst of anger.

'I have told you before, I behave as I wish. I saw you come here. I also saw your face at the cathedral and as you returned to the *castillo*. You are planning to leave me.'

'I am not!' His attitude and his painful grip on her were beginning to allow her temper to rise over any fears. 'I'm not some chicken-hearted schoolgirl. I'm going to marry you, remember? Yes, I'm scared, but it's not a sign that I'm about to break my word. In England I lived a very ordinary life and if I had married David, then someone, even if only a friend, would have led me down the aisle, and it wouldn't have been in some great cathedral where I felt like a rather nervous film star who didn't know her lines. Yes, I'm scared!'

'It is only that? You will face the days of your life as the Condesa de las Montanas and my wife?' He was looking into her eyes as if trying read her soul, his grip tightened to such painful intensity until she protested with a muffled moan.

'I cannot help it,' he groaned. 'I am desperate to keep you. I could never let you go away now.'

'I wouldn't want to.' Laura was certain that for some reason he needed reassurance. This man, this being who made his own rules and decision, had some deep corner in his soul that needed to be calmed and comforted, and her fingers touched his face with a tenderness of their own, her love for him trembling on her lips and almost ready to be admitted aloud.

He looked down at her with surprise, his body beginning to relax from the aggression of seconds before.

'You feel a tenderness for me?' he asked with an almost arrogant amazement.

'I wouldn't dare, Señor Conde,' she retorted, laughing up into his face, her hand daringly smoothing his hair that had fallen in a lock of shining black across his forehead.

His smile was the only reward she could have wanted.

'My sweet Laura,' he whispered. 'I sometimes think that like me you would dare anything. The ceremony is not too long and it will be over before you know it. The rest of our lives is much more important. Look upon it as a bad day at the hospital.'

She laughed aloud, and with one final kiss on her smiling lips Rodrigo left her. Nothing had changed except that she had discovered a chink in the hard armour of his personality and, rather than disturbing her, it made him seem more real, more attainable.

Laura needed all her courage on her wedding day. It dawned bright and hot, as every golden day seemed to do. Maria wept and an endless stream of maids came to whisper and peep at her as she was prepared for the cathedral, so that, by the time she arrived, Laura was as cold as ice in spite of the heat of the day and the long train of her white silk gown.

With her colouring and the white heavy silk of the
gown, the circlet of white gardenias in the silvery fairness
of her hair, she looked astonishing, ethereal, part of a
dream, and tradition was broken as, one after another,
the guests gasped until the whole of the congregation was
turned to watch her walk down the seemingly endless
aisle.

Without even a veil to hide behind, she thought she
would never make it, that she would commit some
outrageous crime, like stumbling. Her chin lifted and her
back straightened and she walked on firmly, although
her legs were trembling. A bad day at the hospital. The
thought brought a secret smile to her lips even though her
eyes were wide and anxious.

Then Rodrigo too turned, his glittering gaze sweeping
her from head to foot before locking with her blue and
terrified eyes. He smiled slowly and walked to meet her,
his hand outstretched, and she remembered his words in
the garden, 'the devil take the traditions', as the Conde
de las Montanas broke every rule and led his bride to the
alter himself.

They returned to the castle for the wedding luncheon,
and to Laura it seemed that the number of guests had
grown, but somehow, it didn't matter at all. Oddly
enough, she was happy, happier than she had ever been
in her life, even though with the ceremony over her
husband had become a dark and alarming stranger
again, his eyes watchful as he moved with her among the
guests. Even with the ceremony over, there was still
formality, ritual, a stateliness to the invited guests that
convinced her that many of them were titled. She tried
not to be daunted by the arrogance of some of the faces,
by the fact that the language flowed smoothly around

her, its speed and fluency cutting her out most of the time. It was impossible to believe that she was now the Condesa de las Montanas, wife of the tall dark Spaniard whose courtesy was constant but unsmiling.

It was Laura who saw the Condesa go quietly away after the toasts and some deep instinct led her to follow. The Condesa was in her suite, so intent on gaining the safety of her own apartment that she had left the door open and Laura was able to slip in quietly behind her and see her slump down in a chair.

'I'm all right.' She turned at the sound of Laura's footsteps, forcing herself upright in the chair, but Laura was not deceived.

'I'm calling the doctor.' She made for the phone, and knew that her instincts had been correct when the Condesa made no move to protest.

It was late in the evening when Laura snapped herself to attention for the tenth time as her eyes again began to close. She had been sitting with Rodrigo for hours in the hospital, the monotonous waiting relieved only by endless cups of coffee and the sound of her own footsteps as she paced the floor.

She could only thank the speed with which Miguel had acted when he had received Rodrigo's permission to go ahead with the preparations for the operation on the day she had made her bargain. The team of heart surgeons had already been there, the equipment waiting, and the Condesa had been taken straight to the theatre.

Rodrigo had been silent all the time, and Laura's fears were twofold as she waited. She could not face losing the Condesa now and if she died, Rodrigo would be like a man turned to ice, he would blame her for the failure even if he never mentioned it again.

She remembered the astonishment of the guests as she had reappeared at her own wedding reception in jeans

and blue checked shirt that had seen better days, all
formality pushed aside as she acted by training and
instinct for the sake of the Condesa. Their amazed
glances had meant nothing to her as she had walked
quickly to Rodrigo to tell him, and he too had abandoned
the reception without a backward glance to follow the
ambulance in his car as Laura sat with the Condesa.

It was that little time in the ambulance alone with the
pale and tired woman that made Laura look now with
love and compassion at the man who scarcely seemed to
realise that she was there.

'I must talk to you, Laura,' the Condesa had said, every
breath difficult.

'No, later. You must rest and keep quiet.'

But the Condesa was too anxious to settle into any
calm and, recognising that some anxiety was disturbing
her more than her own weak condition, Laura had let her
talk.

'Before I go into the hospital, I must tell you about
Rodrigo. If I should die now, you'll never know, and you
must know.' The weak hands had gripped Laura's with
failing strength as the Condesa struggled on. 'I should
have told you before, but I wanted his happiness and I
put it off until after the wedding. I'm not very good at
deceit, but for Rodrigo I would do anything.

'Of course you would,' Laura had soothed. 'Any
mother would do anything for her son.'

'He's not my son.'

The shock had Laura sitting silently as the Condesa
continued.

'Felipe and I met when he was in England at
university. I was very young, my father was one of his
professors and he often came to the house. We fell in love
and he asked me to marry him, but I refused. I already
knew that I would never be able to have children and I

also knew that it was his duty to produce an heir. He went back to Spain and later I heard that he'd married, a girl he had met at some gathering in Madrid. She was English, too; I expect that's why he married her.' She sighed, a shuddering sigh that had Laura worried, but she insisted on carrying on.

'She was a weak and frightened girl, no match for Felipe and in no way capable of being the mistress of the castle. After Rodrigo was born, she took to running away, anywhere to escape the restrictions of the position she couldn't uphold. He was five when she finally left for good, and this time there was no way that Felipe could bring her back—she was killed on the mountain road in one of the flash floods we sometimes get here.

'We still loved each other, Felipe and I, and he came for me. He brought Rodrigo, a dark silent little boy who had understood far more than anyone realised. He felt rejected. He felt that she had deserted him because he meant nothing to her. It took a very long time to make him realise that she just couldn't face the responsibilities of the Castillo del Fuego and the burden of being the Condesa. Finally he understood, but he never mentioned her again. From the first he called me mother in that cool firm voice of his, and he never trusted anyone else who was female. There have been plenty of women in his life, my dear, but no one to bring him happiness. When I saw you, when I saw the effect you had on him, the way you got under his guard, the way you stood up to him, then I hoped for the first time ever. Any desertion would finish his life for ever, Laura.'

'I love him,' Laura said quietly, her heart weeping for the dark silent boy who had become a man alone, happier on his savage horse in the high forests than anywhere else, a man capable of affection only for the woman who had filled the bitter emptiness of his life when he was small and vulnerable. She could see that he had never allowed himself to be vulnerable again. She understood all too clearly why his feelings for her would never be more than desire and perhaps, later, companionship.

Laura glanced across at him now and was startled to find his dark eyes on her.

'Let me send for Eduardo to take you home,' he said quietly. 'You've had a very trying day. You look tired.'

'I'll stay.' She stood and began to pace again. 'We'll soon know one way or the other.' She had to stay, she felt that the rest of her life depended on the Condesa's survival because now she understood Rodrigo's fear of the operation; he couldn't afford to lose the woman who had been his only support throughout his childhood.

It was morning when Laura stirred. The sunlight was shining through a small gap in the curtains and she realised without opening her eyes that she was in bed at the castle. Memories came racing back. The operation had been successful, the Condesa was alive. She could just remember getting into the car after they had been told that they could not see her, and then nothing.

The ringing of the telephone had her opening her eyes quickly and turning her head, but she got no further. Rodrigo was beside her, his dark head on the pillow next to hers, and she watched with a fascination tinged with panic as he stirred at the continuous sound.

With a low groan, he hauled himself up on one elbow and lifted the receiver.

'*Dígame?*' It was like listening to the deep, tired growl of a sleepy tiger, and Laura's eyes ran with frightened appraisal over the smooth brown skin of his back as the silk sheets slid down to his hips. She didn't need to look any further to know that he was wearing nothing under

the scanty cover of the sheet. A quick and alarmed glance
at herself told her that she was not naked. Somehow she
had managed to get into the nightdress that had been
waiting for her, the frothy, white creation that had been
made for the bride of the Conde.

She had no idea what was being said, but the
conversation was long and Rodrigo rolled on to his back,
the phone in his hand as he made the occasional brief
comment. He too suddenly seemed to realise where he
was, because his eyes turned quickly towards her,
capturing and holding her gaze as they faced each other
in the wide, soft bed of the bridal suite.

Eventually he replaced the receiver, his eyes never
leaving hers, and then he turned comfortably on his side
to face her.

'She is all right,' he said softly. 'That was Miguel. She
has had a good night and, although we cannot see her
today, she is recovering rapidly.'

'I—I'm glad.' Laura knew she was watching him like a
frightened child, but there was nothing she could do
about that at the moment. 'How—how did I get here?'

'I carried you here early this morning Señora Condesa,' he said with soft mockery. 'You were exhausted,
asleep when the car reached the *castillo*. I carried you
inside and up to our room. You were, according to Maria,
like a small, fair ghost in my arms.' He said nothing else
and watched her with growing amusement as her eyes
slid from his dark, strong chest to diaphanous white of
her nightdress.

'Did Maria . . .?' Laura began.

'She most certainly did not! She is not allowed in the
bridal suite and well she knows it. Her days as a *dueña* are
over, her self-satisfied importance ended.' Rodrigo
raised one sardonic eyebrow. 'I considered it to be the

duty of the bridegroom to prepare his exhausted bride for bed.'

Her soft blushes were greeted by quiet amusement, and he reached out one lazy finger and trailed it from her neck to the deep shadow between her breasts.

'You grumbled quietly throughout,' he informed her. 'I was greatly tempted to leave your beautiful nightwear on the chair, but you were a great enough temptation as it was, so I struggled to get you into it and then kept strictly to my half of the bed. I cannot say that I have slept well. It is not at all how I intended to spend my wedding night.'

Laura closed her eyes to shut out the excitement of the desire that lay sleepily on his face, her whole body tensing with expectancy, her breathing quickening although he had not yet touched her.

She felt him move and then, with no part of his body in contact, his lips covered hers lightly, teasing her mouth, nibbling her lips, as light as thistledown and as warm as the sunlight. A shiver ran through her and he moved closer, his hand running lightly down her arm, his lips brushing her hot cheeks.

'Don't be frightened, *querida*,' he whispered. 'We want each other; let it happen quietly and slowly, let it grow.' The sound of his voice, deep and soft, and the touch of his gently exploring fingers brought an immediate urgency to her body. Still soft from sleep, she was completely vulnerable, and he was treating her with the gentleness she had dreamed of. Her mouth turned to his, seeking him urgently, but he drew back, only allowing her lips to brush his.

'Slowly, my beautiful Laura,' he whispered. 'Slowly until the fire is blazing.'

His stroking hands moved over her shoulders and he pulled her towards him, sliding aside the straps of the nightdress and cupping her breasts with warm strength, his sensitive fingers bringing the tightly budded nipples to stinging life. Laura gasped at the pain and pleasure of it, and his lips moved to replace his fingers, drawing the hard rosy peaks into the warmth of his mouth as his tongue caressed them. His hands slid to her waist, drawing the nightdress away to give him access to the warm trembling smoothness of her stomach.

She gasped in panic as he drew aside the sheets and lifted his head to gaze with dark, moody eyes at the pale length of her body, smoothing away the white gown and tossing it aside. But he silently calmed her with stroking hands, his head lowering to allow his lips to wander over the silky skin of her waist and hips, kissing and biting gently until she cried out at the feelings that raced through her shuddering body.

'Shh! It's all right,' he said softly, moving to rest lightly over her, his hands on the slender length of her legs, his fingers sliding with infinite tenderness to the warmth of her inner thighs. 'Don't be afraid, my little silver dove, just enjoy your feelings. The same feelings are inside me too. You are not alone.'

He took her mouth with warm insistence, his lips parting hers, his tongue lightly stroking against the inner skin of her lower lips before invading more deeply into the warm sweetness to seek her tongue and move against it with growing urgency.

Laura arched in sudden panic as his fingers moved with sudden possession to the moist heart of her femininity, to touch her where no man had ever invaded, but her panic died as molten gold flooded through her and she relaxed, almost sobbing with pleasure, as his lips stroked hers and his voice murmured comfortingly against her mouth.

For long pleasurable seconds, he stroked and fondled her, his lips burning against hers, his hands waking her body into mindless enjoyment as he moved sensously against her until her moans became an endless plea of desire, her body restless and quivering, striving to belong to the tormentor who drove her to distraction but made her wait so long for his final possession.

She felt a shudder run through his powerful body and with a low groan he moved completely over her, gathering her into the hard strength of his thighs.

'*Por Dios*, come to me!' he gasped, lifting her to meet him as he invaded the warmth and softness of her body with desperate demand.

The pain was momentary, but the pleasure mounted until she was calling his name aloud, moving against him with a willingness that made him cry out as they moved together to a place where time ceased to exist, a place higher than the white crests of the sierras, a place higher than the blue cloudless sky.

Laura drifted back slowly to the white and gold of the bridal suite, aware now of the weight of the dark body that had claimed her own so subtly, so gently, and then so masterfully. Rodrigo stirred in a moment and moved his head against the softness of her breasts, his lips caressing her as his hands gathered her against him and he rolled to his side, drawing her with him.

For a long time he was silent, until she began to imagine that he had not felt the magic that had flooded through her, until she began to feel that in some way she had disappointed him.

'Was—was it all right?' She couldn't keep silent. If she had failed him then she wanted to know.

'All right?' He turned her face and looked down at her as she rested against his shoulder. 'When I first saw you in the forest, when I first looked at the beauty of your face and body, when I first lifted you into my arms, I thought, she will take me to paradise.' His eyes adored her and his lips trailed against the flush of her cheeks. 'I have been to paradise, and it was so wonderful that soon I will go there again with you.'

He laughed softly at her expression, his voice gently teasing.

'We cannot visit the hospital today. There are still guests in the *castillo*, guests that I am not at all anxious to meet. I rather fear that we are trapped in our little world here. What is there to do? We will lie and rest and make repeated trips to the world we have discovered together.'

Laura put her slim arms around him and pulled him against the comfort of her breasts, longing to tell him that she loved him so much but not yet having that kind of courage.

'You are encouraging me, *querida*,' Rodrigo whispered softly, nuzzling against her, his tongue already making exploratory movements against her skin.

'You need encouragement, Señor Conde?' she enquired, laughter in her voice.

'Not when I am within fifty yards of you, Señora Condesa,' he retorted, pulling her fiercely against him.

'Hmm, my little dove you must be hungry. You ate nothing yesterday, or so I was told by your *dueña*. Soon I will ring for a huge breakfast and we will eat here together, but first I will satisfy a hunger that food will not help in the slightest.'

She moved with ready acquiescence against him, already anxious to belong to him again, knowing that this time she would meet no gentle encouragement, no tender murmurings, the hard urgency of his body giving her certain knowledge that this time he would take her to the edge of the world with the passionate force of his forefathers.

The night-black eyes that looked down into hers told the same story. For magical moments he had been a considerate lover, but now he was filled with a need to own her body and soul.

'You are mine!' he said thickly, 'Mine to take and keep, mine to bear my child and walk beside me until we die. If you leave me ever, I will find you and kill you!'

Her momentary fear was crushed as his lips took hers in a deep punishing kiss, a kiss that never ended until his harsh uneven breathing steadied against her breast and her languorous body lay fulfilled and bruised beneath the weight of his. He had taken her as if some devil possessed him, and the eyes that looked up slowly into hers admitted it and showed no regret.

'You know now that you are mine for all your days?' he asked with a harsh demand.

'I know, Rodrigo,' she acknowledged, and his eyes softened and shadowed with hidden pain when she wound her arms around his neck and kissed the dark moist hair that fell against his forehead.

'I am in your net as you are in mine,' he breathed, his arms enclosing her gently. 'We will live together and die together, *pequeña*, but we will never be apart.'

'That is all I ask, Rodrigo,' she assured him softly. 'Just to be with you and to try my best every day to please you.'

'How could you not?' he enquired softly, his eyes scanning her face for something that he had searched for before. Laura closed her eyes to defeat him. It would be madness to tell him of her love. Already he gripped her soul and that would have to be enough. Perhaps one day, when they had children, when she felt secure in her role and in her marriage, perhaps then she would tell him and drive the devil away for ever.

'I think that it is time to feed you,' he said with a return to lightheartedness, swinging lithely from the bed and pulling her with him. 'You may shower first, Condesa, and I will arrange the menu.'

Her blushes as his eyes slid over her naked body set him laughing again and he turned her to the bathroom with a quick slap on her bottom.

'I can promise to cure you of blushing in no time at all,' he assured her. 'If you wait, we will shower together.'

His laughter was lingering in her ears as she grasped her white gown and fled.

CHAPTER TEN

IT was several days later, on the way back from visiting the Condesa in hospital, that Laura sat in silence beside Rodrigo in the luxury of the Mercedes. The wooded road to the castle was always a delight to her. From the main highway, it fell in sweeping curves to the lower edge of the forest and then wound through secret arches of trees to the imposing front gates.

Glancing at her, Rodrigo slowed the car and leaned back comfortably, his glittering eyes watchful and assessing as they travelled beneath the sun-splashed arches of greenery.

'You like this stretch of road, no?'

'Mmm,' she nodded, and smiled. 'It's so secret and — well—secure.'

'You feel secure with me?' His eyes were hooded, as mysterious as the forest around them, and Laura turned away, hiding her own face.

'Why shouldn't I? We're married. I'm adjusting to the grand life.'

She hadn't meant any criticism, any sharp rejoinder, but as she heard his breath sucked sharply in, she realised that he had taken it like that.

'I am not talking about material things, about concrete things. I asked if you felt secure with me.' He glanced at her with tightened lips, his eyes cool. 'I realise that you have a good line in self-control, but I think that often you are very withdrawn. How long will it be, Laura, before we blend in our daily lives as well as we blend at night?'

Her flushed cheeks seemed merely to irritate him and

he shot her a glance of exasperation mixed with what in anyone else she would have taken for despair.

Often, since their wedding night, she had caught that look on his face, a hidden, barely visible misery. It disappeared soon enough in the fiery emotion that came so swiftly when they touched, but many times throughout the day she would feel his eyes on her and look up to see an icy blackness that seemed to be the mirror of his soul. Then she felt her own inadequacies only too well, then she realised that no one could ever hold his heart except for the one corner of it that had been given to the Condesa.

He was anxious to be free, to be out on Diablo in the lonely beauty of the foothills, seeking his own kind of peace. If he had loved her, it would have been different— but he didn't, he had never pretended to.

There was nothing she could say, and they swept through the gates and under the great stone arch in a bleak silence. There were few quarrels between them now because any friction was firmly squashed by Rodrigo. At the first sign of any dissension he made love to her, swift, fiery and utterly subduing. After that Laura never felt like opposing him; the magic lingered too long and it was easy to forget that there had been any dispute.

'What the hell is she doing here?' His sudden exclamation took her by surprise.

'Who?' As far as she could see, there was no one in sight. The great courtyard was empty, sunlight in every corner.

'Carlota! She went into the stables. I would know that hideous bright green blouse she sometimes wears if the day were foggy and dim. I saw her!'

He brought the car to a purring halt, jumping out and coming swiftly to open Laura's door.

'Go inside!' It was a sharp order and he turned

abruptly, making for the stables without another glance in her direction. Whatever he had seen, he was determined to investigate, and he was angry. Laura felt he must be mistaken and she began to cross to the huge doors of the *castillo*, but her feet dragged more slowly as she went as a feeling of grave disquiet began to replace her surprise.

She felt almost fey, every instinct on the alert, swamping her so much that she turned suddenly to follow Rodrigo, sure without any good reason that there was danger.

She had taken only a few steps when a hoarse cry from the stables shocked her into immobility. She never had the chance to go forward because, with a wild clatter of hooves, Diablo surged through the darkness of the open doors and out into the sunlight.

He looked like some vision from hell, his black coat gleaming, his eyes wide and staring, his head tossing in a frenzy. For a second he looked around, seemingly intent on escape, but the Mercedes blocked the exit through the arch, parked as Rodrigo had left it in his haste to investigate, and Laura made the mistake of moving. He saw her instantly and bore down on her with the speed of his thoroughbred ancestry. Only one thought was in her mind.

'He means to kill me!'

She knew that if she turned and ran, he would run her down; his bared teeth made his intentions plain. Once in her childhood she had seen a horse attack like this and she knew that there would be no escape unless she could somehow halt the headlong rush. She saw Rodrigo erupt from the stables, two grooms behind him, but he would never be there in time; she had to keep her nerve.

At the last minute she acted, shouting and flinging up her arms, waving her shoulder bag wildly, and for a

second the horse stopped, his eyes red-tinged and rolling.
As she had expected, he reared, lashing out with deadly
hooves, towering over her, screaming in a way that she
had never imagined possible with an animal. He seemed
to have gone mad.

She rolled, avoiding the murderous hooves by inches
as they struck the stone of the wall. She could never
manage that again, he was too fast, too clever, but as he
backed and prepared to rear again. Rodrigo arrived.

White-faced and murderous himself, aggression in
every muscle of his powerful frame, he did the only thing
possible, charging in like a bolt of thunder, his strong
shoulder to the point of Diablo's shoulder, the place
chosen with the skill of years of horsemanship, and the
great horse staggered and fell.

They were on him in an instant, Rodrigo on his
massive neck, the groom who ran the stables pulling off
his belt and lashing it around the fetlock, immobilising
the frenzied horse before he could recover and rise.

'The rifle!' Rodrigo leapt up, hand outstretched to take
the heavy hunting rifle carried by the second groom, and
for a minute Laura stood stunned. Seconds ago she had
been facing death, and now the beautiful brute on the
ground faced certain destruction.

Diablo was struggling to rise but unable to gain any
purchase, with one leg bent and fastened securely. Still he
was in a frenzy of rage, his head tossing wildly, the
magnificient black mane damp and matted with sweat—
and something else!

'Wait! Rodrigo, wait!' Laura ran forward, avoiding
the bared teeth and ignoring Rodrigo's sharp cry of
warning, grasping Rodrigo's arm and pointing to the
blood that now gushed from beneath the matted gloss of
Diablo's mane. Then they all saw what her sharp eyes
had seen—the haft of a dagger protruding from the

powerful neck, half hidden beneath the heavy fall of hair, the black gold-embossed haft proclaiming its origin. They had all seen it before; it was one of a pair that had been mounted with other relics of the warlike past of the Montanas, and the last time Laura had seen it had been in the great hall as she had studied the weapons there with awestricken eyes.

Rodrigo pulled it free, swearing in Spanish with such fluency that at any other time Laura felt her ears would have caught fire. Luckily she did not understand, but she caught the gist and even the grooms looked startled. As the horse gave a long shuddering moan, they all knew what had driven him to murder.

'Poor, poor thing!' Laura quickly held her handkerchief as a pad to the flow of blood as the horse turned his head.

'Laura!' Rodrigo was not fast enough to stop her holding her flat hand to the velvet nostrils that searched towards her, but his anxiety was needless. The madness was over and Diablo blew softly into her hand, accepting the soothing palm as it moved to his neck.

'*Dios!* If you dare to risk yourself again like that I will shake you into insensibility!' roared Rodrigo, jerking her to her feet, but she escaped from his anger easily, falling in a dead faint at his feet as he released her.

She came round to find herself on the softness of the bed, her head throbbing with pain.

'You grazed your head.' Rodrigo stayed her searching fingers, replacing the compress he had been holding to her forehead. 'You were a little too quick for me. I can see why you need a stiff white cap,' he joked shakily.

'You didn't shoot Diablo?' she whispered anxiously.

'No' He shook his head. 'You told me to wait and I am waiting. He is calm and normal. Clearly the pain drove him to such madness, but he tried to kill you. He is no longer to be trusted.'

'I don't want you to destroy him,' she whispered, the pain, the shock, and her love for Rodrigo bringing tears to her eyes.

'I cannot risk your life, but we will discuss it later.' He was sitting on the bed beside her and his thumb wiped the tears away with rough tenderness. 'Why did you stop me? It would have been over now. You risked your life again by coming close. Why?'

'You—you love him,' she said quietly, turning her head away, tears still falling. 'I know what he means to you. Eduardo said you were only at peace on Diablo, riding in the forest. I—I know these past few days you've been longing to go.'

'You risked yourself to save an animal because you imagine that I care for him?' Rodrigo stared at her with a strange expression in his eyes that she could in no way understand. 'You thought I would shoot him and then grieve, never be at peace again? You thought that this was worth your life? Why, *por Dios*!'

Laura closed her eyes, unable to look at him, waiting for his anger, waiting for him to tell her that she had duties too great to risk herself in any way.

'You need him,' she whispered, shaken by silent weeping. 'I couldn't bear it if you lost him and had so much heartache.'

'Why, Laura?' He gripped her hands in an almost savage hold. 'Why must I have no heartache?'

'I love you.' She turned despairing eyes, swimming with tears, to meet his dark gaze as bravely as she could. 'I know what you think of love. I know you don't want me to love you. I—I know you'll never love me, but I don't care. I love you and it's enough.'

'It is not enough!' He almost shouted the words at her

and then lifted her gently into his arms, afraid to hurt her. '*Querida!* You imagine that I don't need your love? That I don't want it?' His eyes adored her and her heart leapt again at the sight of so much worship. 'I have needed it since I first saw you, since I stood stunned and humbled at the sight of your perfection—so fair, so beautiful, so far from my grasp. I knew then why I had sidestepped my obligations, why I had never married. I had waited for my dream, for the other half of myself.' He rocked her gently and looked down into her wide blue eyes, glistening with tears but beginning to shine with happiness. 'My love,' he whispered, 'I was so afraid. We are so different in so many ways, you and I. *Sol y sombra*, from two different worlds. You had a career, a settled life that did not include me, that left no room for me; but I had to have you, to get you in any way possible.' He laughed softly, teasing her willing lips with his. 'You showed from the first a stubborn determination to follow your own path, but there was fear in your eyes as you saw me and I knew that, if you realised that I had fallen in love with you on sight, you would leave Spain so fast that I would have spent the rest of my life chasing around to find you. I saw your sparkling eyes, your determined little chin, and then I had it! I knew that if I intimated that I wished you to leave, you would be determined to stay, from sheer . . .'

'Contrariness?' Laura helped, smiling into his eyes.

'It is a good word?' he asked cautiously.

'It describes my reaction to you fairly well,' she laughed softly, tracing the beloved face with her fingertips. 'But Eduardo said . . .'

'Eduardo does not know everything, my love. All he knew was that you were here. I rang him in Córdoba and said only one sentence, "I have found her". He came back very speedily to have a look at you. I imagine that

anything he said was to gain your sympathy for me, and I
needed it.' Rodrigo smiled into her eyes. 'This horse that
I need so badly I have not ridden once since the day I
found you, except for the time that we went together in
the forest. The grooms have complained bitterly that
they have had to exercise him, but I could not leave the
castillo; you were here and that is where I wanted to be.'

He sighed deeply and trailed his lips softly against her
cheeks.

'Every day I have loved you more. When I make love
to you, I worship you silently. When I look at you I have
everything I need. If I have your love then I have
paradise; there is no word, no expression to tell you how I
feel. When Miguel has looked at your head, when you are
better, I will show you how I love you.'

He put her gently back against the pillows, looking
down at her with a sudden frown of determination.

'As to Diablo, I will get another horse.'

'No!' Laura struggled to get up. 'I want you to keep
him. Anything in pain is likely to go mad for a while.
He'll like me in the end. I'll get the better of him yet.'

'Don't you always get the better of us all?' Rodrigo put
her firmly back against the soft pillows, his lips hovering
over hers. 'I can think of no one in the *castillo* who is not
now firmly under your control and who does not love it—
I most of all. I would be happy if you ground me under
your heel.'

'Oh Rodrigo,' she sighed, just before his lips silenced
her. 'You lie so beautifully, so poetically.'

'It is the Latin blood, *querida*,' he murmured against
her lips. 'I imagine that it will grow on you rapidly.'

Having been pronounced fit, and berated soundly by
Miguel Hernandes for taking risks, Laura was settled
comfortably in bed by Maria, who had been allowed to

fuss over her for a while as Rodrigo went back to the stables. When he returned his face was thunderous. He looked determined and bent on retribution.

'It was Carlota,' he growled at her enquiry. 'Did I not tell you that I had seen the flash of that tasteless blouse? She entered the stables saying that she would ride while waiting for us and that she would saddle her own horse. Left to herself she had time to get up to any kind of mischief. I saw her as she was running out; her car was probably parked off the forest track. Perhaps we even passed it. I will see her tomorrow and ask how she would like to spend some time in Mexico. Her relatives are there—I think she will prefer them to a long stay in prison.'

He stormed off to take a shower, and Laura thanked heaven that she was not Carlota. As an enemy Rodrigo was deadly, and she knew he would not spare the Spanish girl when Diablo had tried to kill her. It was just as likely that the murderous attack had been aimed at Rodrigo, though, and thinking that, Laura did not feel inclined to intervene, although she could see on his face that any attempt at intervention would be useless. He was once again her master, arrogant and domineering.

She was sitting up in bed, the lamplight soft on her face, when he came back, still frowning from the shower, but his frown left him as he saw her.

'You have a headache still, my darling?' he enquired softly, and when she shook her head, he added quietly, 'then why are you so silent and thoughtful? You have discovered that you do not love me after all?'

Although he was joking, there was even so an anxiety in his eyes, and Laura held out her arms to him, allowing her love to show so clearly that he could never doubt it.

'There's something we must discuss,' she told him

quietly. 'We must get all our thoughts, our worries, our
doubts into the open.'

Rodrigo drew back and looked at her guardedly,
standing again and looking down at her so seriously that
her heart quaked, but she had to bring any secret out into
the light, there must be no shadow over them.

'I know about your mother, Rodrigo. The Condesa
told me when she thought she might die. Would you like
to talk about it?'

'No!' He turned away stiffly and then spun back with
narrowed eyes. 'Is this why you profess to love me? Is this
why I must suffer no hurt again? The nurse in you is
coming out and you are sorry for me?'

'When you are here, I don't feel like a nurse, Rodrigo,'
Laura said quietly, facing his doubt and anger. 'I feel like
a woman first and a nurse second, as you once advised
me to feel. I suppose I feel a pity for you,' she added
honestly, 'but that's only because I love you too much.
You have a mother, one who has loved you since you
were a tiny boy, and just because she did not give birth to
you she is still nevertheless your mother. The very act of
having a child does not necessarily make anyone a
mother; love does that, not some biological function. I
suppose I should feel more sorry for myself. I never knew
my mother and now my father is dead I have no one.'

'You have me!' Rodrigo came forward and pulled her
up to her knees, his hands tight and possessive. 'You
need no one else. I love you enough for a dozen families!'

'And that's how I love you,' she said softly, ignoring
the pain of his grasp. 'I want no more mourning inside
about a woman you hardly knew, a woman you scarcely
remember. You have a beautiful mother who will now
live and you have a wife who adores you. No more
darkness, Rodrigo, let's have less of the *sombra* and more
of the *sol*.'

'You cunning little creature!' His smile grew slowly until it lit up the whole of his happy face. 'You use my weapons against me. You drive me to jealousy when you tell me that you have no one and then neatly turn it around. I will have to sharpen my wits if I am to remain master and control my little silver bird.' His arms went round her and she tilted her face to laugh into his eyes, her body beginning to burn at his touch, her breathing to quicken until they were gazing deeply at each other, unsmiling, a longing beginning to grow inside them both.

'Who put you into this alluring nightdress?' he murmured against her lips. 'You know I will only toss it on the carpet.'

'Maria helped me to bed,' she breathed shakily. 'I didn't feel up to making explanations, so I just let her have her way.'

'And now you will let me have my way?' he enquired wickedly.

'Can I stop you?' she smiled, her lips teasing the dark skin of his throat as he stroked the nightdress from her.

'You can always fight me, *adorata*, but I suspect that I would enjoy that too,' he whispered, the nightdress tossed aside, his hands roaming over her silken skin with growing pleasure.

'Mmm. Now you are no surprise to me when I touch you,' he whispered. 'Now I know every part of you and every part of you is mine. I caress you now with the memory of the past, the joy of the present and the thrill of the future.'

'You're so beautiful,' Laura sighed, kneeling against him, her hands untying his bathrobe and sliding it from him.

'I? Beautiful?' He drew back and smiled in surprise.

'Perfect,' she assured him, her lips trailing softly across the bronzed skin of his hard chest. 'Like a dark god from the forest. Beautiful, exciting and perfect. Do you think our children will be like you? Real Montanas? Dark and powerful?'

'We will have to see, who knows such things?' he murmured, pushing her gently down into the silken sheets and joining her. 'There is only one way to find out, and I grow more impatient to know by the second.'

It was several months later when Rodrigo walked quietly in the walled gardens with Laura, his arm around her shoulders, his eyes looking with a quiet happiness at the sunlit castle walls, the fountains and the trees tossing in the light breeze. Autumn had turned to winter and winter into spring. The snow on the high sierras had melted to swell the sparkling streams and the castle glistened in the late sunlight.

'Wait!' He pulled her back behind the security of a thick hedge as she moved to rejoin the Condesa, who sat with Eduardo and Miguel on the patio. 'I do not want to share you yet. I still suspect Miguel Hernandes; even now I rather think that he loves you. He wanted you for himself and you're mine, both of you are mine,' he added possessively, his hands sliding gently over the rounded swell of her stomach.

'He now has a very professional interest in me,' Laura told him severely, turning to look into his dark, determined eyes. 'If you feel like that, then we'd better have another doctor for the event, but you'd better be quick to decide—these things can't be ignored.'

'No, my sweet,' Rodrigo repented softly. 'He is the best. I am just perhaps too possessive. You forgive me?'

'I love it!' she laughed. 'I get all my own way, I'm spoiled and fussed over. Sometimes I have to hide from your mother and Maria.

'Are you tired?' he asked anxiously. 'I will carry you.'

'Both of us?' she mocked, her eyes wide with surprise.

'Both of you, my beautiful one,' he assured her. 'If you are not tired, however, I thought we might watch the fires.'

Laura was only too anxious to see the spectacle again. It was so long since she had stood with Rodrigo and watched the flickering colours cross the castle walls, and somehow or other she had never seen them again. Life was so full, so rich, that time flew by happily and the days blended into each other, every one more joyous and fulfilling than the next.

'Why were you so hateful to me when you brought me here to see them the first time?' she asked, suddenly remembering their quarrel following the first and only time they had stood together watching the magic of the fires as they stood now.

'Ah! It was very necessary that you should not see the end of the fires,' he confessed, pulling her close and turning her back to see the castle walls awash with brilliant lights.

'I'm staying now!' she said determinedly.

'It is perfectly safe for you to see them now,' he murmured. 'You are mine in no uncertain way,' he added with a low laugh.

'I think I'd like to hear this mysterious reason, please,' Laura insisted, and he began with no reluctance.

'It is the legend, my love,' he explained. 'As you know, there are many legends and traditions in such an old family, in such an old *castillo*, but the legend of the fires is the most powerful one. When the Conde de las Montanas falls in love, his beloved must never see the end of the fires until she is his alone. It is said that if she does, then he will never have his own true love. I hastened you into the *castillo* with more vigour than courtesy when you wished to see the end of the fires because of the legend.'

'You really loved me, even then?' Laura enquired dreamily.

'As I saw you, *encantadora*, as my eyes looked at you my heart adored you,' he murmured against her silvery hair.

'Why, Rodrigo, you're superstitious!' she teased, looking up at him, and his eyes flashed in their exciting way, dark and glittering.

'Not really,' he smiled. 'We are after all in the twentieth century. But still, it is better to be safe than sorry, no?'

'Did the Condesa know about the fires?' Laura asked, leaning against the strength of the man who held her in gentle strong arms.

'Certainly! She is, how do you say, big on traditions.'

'I wish I'd asked her,' Laura sighed. 'I would have known so much sooner that you loved me.'

'And you would have led me a greater dance than you did already, 'Rodrigo said firmly. 'In any case, she would not have been willing to tell you. You hold the secret now as you hold the betrothal ring for just a little while longer. When our son is a man I will tell him, and you, my dove, will be sworn to secrecy until he is safely married.'

'It may be a girl, fair like me,' Laura teased softly. 'What then, Señor Conde?'

'I will have two silver doves. What more could a man ask?' he said quietly, his lips teasing her earlobe. 'Then also we will have to try really hard to produce a male heir to the estates, no matter how many attempts it takes,' he added seductively. 'It will be my pleasure, Condesa.'

He turned her in his arms, his lips capturing her smiling mouth, his hands gentle on her blushing cheeks.

'If there had been no chance whatever of an heir,' he whispered softly, 'then still you would have been my love, still you would have shared my life as the Condesa de las

Montanas. I am doubly lucky that we are so—compatible, but you are all I need, you are my whole life.

Their long kiss was broken as he turned her back to the castle, holding her safely as they watched the fires fade and die as the sun dipped behind the highest snow-capped peak of the mountains, and there was nothing more that Laura wanted than the love of the tall powerful Spaniard who had stormed into her life and captured her heart. Her days would be filled with duty as the Condesa de las Montanas, but her nights would be filled with love and their future was sealed. What more could she desire?

Sarah

MAURA SEGER

Sarah wanted desperately to escape the clutches of her cruel father.
Philip needed a mother for his son, a mistress for his plantation.
It was a marriage of convenience.
Then it happened. The love they had tried to deny suddenly became a
blissful reality. . . only to be challenged by life's hardships and brutal
misfortunes.

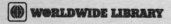
SAR-1